A Garland Series

The Feminist Controversy
in England 1788-1810

A collection of 44 interesting
and important works reprinted
in photo-facsimile in 89 volumes

edited by

Gina Luria

Rutgers University

Azemia

A Descriptive and Sentimental Novel

William Beckford

In Two Volumes

Vol. II

with an introduction
for the Garland edition by
Gina Luria

Garland Publishing, Inc., New York & London

1974

Bibliographical note:

This facsimile has been made from a copy in the
Beinecke Library of Yale University
(Im.B388.797A)

Library of Congress Cataloging in Publication Data

Beckford, William, 1760-1844.
   Azemia; a descriptive and sentimental novel interspersed with pieces of poetry.

   (The Feminist controversy in England, 1788-1810)
   Reprint of the 1797 ed. printed by and for S. Low,
London.
      I. Title. II. Series.
PZ3.B389Az5 [PR4091]   823'.6   74-8006
ISBN 0-8240-0850-2

AZEMIA.

VOL. II.

AZEMIA:

A DESCRIPTIVE AND SENTIMENTAL

NOVEL.

INTERSPERSED WITH PIECES OF POETRY.

By JACQUETTA AGNETA MARIANA JENKS,

OF BELLEGROVE PRIORY IN WALES.

DEDICATED TO

THE RIGHT HONORABLE LADY HARRIET MARLOW.

TO WHICH ARE ADDED,

CRITICISMS ANTICIPATED.

IN TWO VOLUMES.

VOL. II.

No flimfy gauze and frippery fcenes I wrote,
With patches here and there like Jofeph's coat.
CHURCHILL.

London:

PRINTED BY AND FOR

SAMPSON LOW, NO. 7, BERWICK STREET, SOHO.

1797.

AZEMIA.

CHAPTER I.

He is a man, take him for all in all,
We ne'er fhall look upon his like again.

SHAKESPEARE.

" YET fo faid Timothy Twaddle—
that good, faithful, excellent old fervant,
Timothy Twaddle, told me that fhe
loved."

Such was the foliloquy of the Rev. Solomon Sheeppen, meditating on Azemia's
difappearance, as he *galloped ventre à
terre* between Royfton and London. A
turnpike gate fuddenly intercepted his
dangerous career; but fuch was the agi-
tation of his mind (for which a flying
leap has often proved a fpecific), that
he was on the point of taking it—when
the turnpike man, Walter Waglock,
who was fettling a point about a dif-
puted three-pence half-penny (with
Jack Jerkin, a poft-boy at the Angel at
Royfton), ftepped forward, for he took
Mr. Sheeppen for a highwayman; when
fuddenly recollecting him, for he had
known him ever fince he was an under
graduate, he faid,

" Good

" Good lack ! why, what is the matter
with you, Reverend Sir ?—Leap over
fuch a turnpike-gate as this here?—Why,
Lord ! it would go nigh to break your
neck."

Sheeppen now perceiving Waglock,
faid in a faint voice, " Take your money, Mafter Walter, and let me pafs:
I have not a moment to lofe." He
fpoke in a voice of extreme fenfibility.

The turnpike man would probably
have been affected even to tears had
he heard him, but he was prevented by
the extreme jingling of the Newmarket
waggon that moment approaching.
Sheeppen ftruck, however, his horfe,
and purfued his journey, in a difpofition of mind hard to be defcribed, to-

wards

wards Enfield ;—then gently galloping, and more tardily trotting, through Edmonton, he paffed the ever-memorable fign of the Bell, where he gave a fentimental figh to the gayer adventures of John Gilpin, envying his celebrity, while he regretted the days that were gone, when the involuntary excurfion to Ware of the juftly-celebrated linen-draper could enwreathe his cheeks with a fmile.

" It is not fo *now*," faid he: " Love, unhappy love, has obfcured aʜ my profpects, and blighted the bloomy bloffoms of benevolent beatitude. In vain for me now would be all the luxuriant lufcioufnefs of lavifh nature. Though the fun fhould diffufe its moft *splendid* glories over the *grateful*
bofom

bosom of the *humid* earth, and the *moist-eyed* moon should melt in her *mellifluous* meridian: though *wild* geese, or even wild *ducks*, teal, and widgeon, should glide glittering over the gay and *gauzy* water, *begemmed* with lilies, and reflecting the weeping willow whispering over its waving way: though easterlings, or even coots and dabchicks, should sweep its lucid surface with their enamelled pinions; and though dulcet music of mountain breezes, and hollow sounds of falling cascades, should unite to whisper delicate dreams of dawning delight!—all! all would be in vain! — Even the distant prospect of Winchmore Hill, hiding its *blue* head in the severing clouds that float in feathery festoons — the citizens in their whiskeys—the lower ranks in their plea-

B 3   sure

fure carts — even directors and rich
merchants in their handfome coaches,
bounding and *frifking* along thefe well-
kept roads, that lead the amufed eye
towards Newington and Kingfland on
one fide ; on the other, diverging towards Clapton, Homerton, and Hackney : the intermingling notes of wood-
land melody, from the flower-befprin-
kled hedge-rows ; all prefenting a picture, exquifitely fublime, yet foothe
not the fad foul of Solomon Sheeppen!
Alas! *he* feels that nothing *can* foothe
it, or betray it a moment from the
contemplation of the graces of Azemia : fhe has indeed

" Murdered fleep."

Thus faying, he turned his horfe to the
left, determining, though he knew not
why,

why, to take the Hackney road to London; but when he reached the Mermaid (celebrated in political annals for Middlefex meetings), he felt himfelf fo entirely overcome by a fenfe of his loft happinefs, that he was compelled to enter, and call for a difh of poached eggs.

While he waited for this refreshment, he took up, in that carelefs way one does at an inn, a newfpaper that lay on the window feat: it was the Sun—a paper remarkable for difinterefted candour and ungarbled fimplicity of narrative, as well as for the elegant purity of its Englifh, and the admirable accuracy of its tranflations from that language become *fo* deteftable from the *exifting circumftances* of the na-

tion·

tion which fpeaks it, that it is *toafted againft* by fome of the moft *manly* and *unblemifhed* charaɛters of *modern old England.*

He gazed moft lackadaifically upon it, " unknowing what he fought," till the poetry, always fo taftefully feleɛted, attraɛted his attention : that which immediately prefented itfelf was a Sonnet—it was of the melancholy caft—it was pathetic — it was touching—it was appropriate—and it vibrated for a moment on all the ftrings and fources of fympathetic fenfibility, as Mr. Sheeppen read thus :

SONNET

SONNET

TO DARKNESS.

Oh ! Darkneſs !' hide me with thine ebon ray *,
And let thy brown ſhade o'er my boſom drop,
Guard my ſad boſom from the torch of day,
And bid thy chills my hurrying pulſes ſtop ;
While in thy glimmering gloom I gladly wrap
My temples, and attune the ſoul-ſad lay !
Reclining on the meadow's breathing crop
Of bos-befriending † flower-beſprinkled hay ;

---

   * A *ray* of darkneſs is a new image ; at leaſt I recollect only two modern poets who uſe it. It gives me an idea ſo perfectly obſcure, that I perſuade myſelf it is what Milton means by darkneſs viſible.

   † " Bos-befriending." The Italian ſcholar will know how to appreciate this expreſſive compound epithet. It is hardly neceſſary to explain it, even to female readers.

Or 'neath the verdant fhade of cyprefs ftop,
To hear fweet Philomel falute the May.
Come, gentle Darknefs, in thy veil of jet
Enwreathe me, votary of the moift-eyed mufe!
So in thy raven robe I may forget
Pearlina *! and drink deep oblivious dews.

The congeniality of the fentiment re-
conciled our clerical wanderer for once,
to what he had, on fo many occafions,
and particularly in his difputes with
Iphaniffa, defcribed as the fenfelefs
fuavity of fentimental fimplicity, or the
piping plaintivenefs of parading pathos.
Befides, this being a legitimate fonnet,

* Pearlina is a name derived from pearls, appli-
cably applied as a comparative and an emendative
either to the fkin or the teeth of the Fair. The
Italians have feveral names derived from gems; as
Diamantina—Opalina, for a capricious beauty, &c.

and

and upon the Italian model, it was,
he owned, a fhade, a degree better and
more claffical than the poetic baftards
obtruded upon the public tafte, " even
to fatiety." Scarce had he finifhed this
internal critique, when roufing himfelf
from the weak indulgence of the ener-
vating paffion of love, he ate his eggs
with an appetite worthy of a curate who
has ferved five churches; then called
for fome more newfpapers to amufe his
mind from the fad fubject of his contemplations, while he digefted them.
All his love-enwoven thoughts, and
even the bright image of Azemia, faded
from his recollection as he read the following animated Ode in another of the
conftellation of *Suns* that were brought
to him, and recognized the elegant and
fpirited hand of his long-efteemed
          B 6   friend,

friend, and some time fellow student, Mr. Paridel Puffwell, now an Under Secretary of State.

ODE, PANEGYRICAL AND LYRICAL.

TO THE TUNE OF HOSIER'S GHOST.

YE, who places hold, or pensions,
    And as much as ye can get,
Come, and hear the praising mention
    I shall make of Mister Pitt.

All he does is grand and daring,
    All he says is right and fit;
Never let us then be sparing
    In the praise of Mister Pitt.

Who, like him, can prate down reason*,
    Who so well on taxes hit?
Who detect a plot of treason
    Half so well as Mister Pitt?

---

* Not reason according to the vulgar acceptation of the word, but false reasoning founded on democratic data, which is of course no reason at all. The word occurs here merely for the *rhythm*.

He's

He's the man to make thefe nations
   Own their millions of debit—
Well incurr'd, as prove orations
   Duly made by Mifter Pitt.

That he's prov'd a great financier,
   'Tis as true as holy writ ;
He's a *rate* and *duty fancier* *,
   Heaven-born tax-man—Mifter Pitt.

Oppofition try to hurt him,
   Only in his place to fit ;
Let *us* not, my friends, defert him,
   Stick ye clofe to Mr. Pitt.

---

* Certain mechanics fome years ago formed themfelves into inoffenfive affociations, called Fanciers' clubs : fome were pigeon fanciers, fome felt emulation about the feathered properties of canary birds. Happy times ! happy men ! when *fedition fancying* was unknown, and no man dreaded the Mum Acts. Much are fuch employments to be recommended.——*Note by Mr. Reeve.*

He

He the multitude is humbling,
  Britons that doth well befit:
Swinish crowds, who minds your grumbling?
  Bow the knee to Mister Pitt.

Tho' abroad our men are dying,
  Why should he his projects quit?
What are orphans, widows, crying,
  To our steady Mister Pitt?

His is fortitude of mind, Sir:
  That remark do not omit;
He by Heaven was design'd, Sir,
  To humble England——Glorious Pitt!

You ne'er see him love a wench, Sir,
  Driving curricle and tit;
He attends the Treasury-bench, Sir,
  Sober, honest, Mister Pitt.

What cares he for Fox's raving,
  Or for Sherry's caustic wit?
Still the *nation* he keeps shaving,
  Pretty close too——Mister Pitt!

Two

Two thirds of that nation ftarving,
    Now of meat ne'er tafte a bit;
For his friends he ftill is carving,
    This great ftatefman—Mifter Pitt.

Mifter Pitt has elocution
    Greater far than John De Witt*;
Give up then our Conftitution,
    As advifes Mifter Pitt.

He *out-herods* Oppofition,
    Heedlefs he of every fkit †;
For the ftate a rare phyfician,
    To bleed and fweat, is Mifter Pitt.

Britons once were *too* victorious,
    And they love it too much yet;
Humility is far more glorious,
    As 'tis taught by Mifter Pitt.

---

* A Dutchman, whofe intentions were miftaken, and who fuffered unjuftly from popular prejudice.

† A cant word for the paltry effufions of party malice, exhibited at elections, &c.

Lo!

Lo! fresh millions he will raise, Sir,
   Tho' we don't advance a whit;
Give him then imperial praise, Sir,
   Viva viva Mister Pitt!

Praise him, all ye Treasury Genii!
   That he's wrong, Oh! ne'er admit;
Fear not Fox's honest keen-eye,
   While ye stick to Mister Pitt.

Laud him, Bishops, Deans, and Prebends,
   All by inspiration lit;
Praise him, blue and crimson ribands,
   Knights! bepraise your patron Pitt.

Stretch your throats, ye fat Contractors,
   He employs your pot and spit;
Laugh at impotent detractors,
   Envying you and Mister Pitt.

New-made Lords shall join the song, Sirs,
   Nor will Rose or Steele forget
To declaim, or right or wrong, Sirs,
   In the praise of Mister Pitt.

                    Oh!

Oh! berhyme him, courtly writers!
  Nares and Gifford, men of wit;
Pye, and all ye ode-inditers,
  Strike your lyres to Mifter Pitt!

Learn, each *Jacobin* Reviewer,
  Analytical or Crit.;
Learn from *Britifh* Critics, truer,
  To appreciate Mifter Pitt.

So a chorus fhall arife, Sir,
  That the welkin's brows fhall hit;
Britons' joyous *grateful* cries, Sir,
  Shall be heard thro' earth and fkies, Sir,
And the univerfe furprife, Sir,
  In honour of the heaven-born Pitt *.

Struck with the truth and elevated
fentiments of this admirable piece of
                   poetry,

* In fome *low* Jacobin prints, which impertinently
copied this *adulatory* ode, another verfe was foifted
                         in,

poetry,, Mr. Sheeppen (himself truly
miniſterial from principle and con-
viction, and having been bred among,
the ſuccefsfully *booing* candidates for
mitres, &c.) mounted his horſe, and
animated with the genuine love of the
good things of his country, he determined to wait on Dr. Prettyman, Biſhop
of Lincoln, the very next day, to ſolicit
a living in his gift, not far from Bugden;
once more began galloping; and ſoon,

---

in, worthy of the vulgar and dirty preſs it iſſued
from—I print it merely to ſhew that it is ſurrepti-
tious—it follows in thoſe diſcreditable papers,
verſe 15.

> Chatham's blood he is belying,
>   Teaching Britons to ſubmit;
> But, perhaps the D—— flying
>   Might *produce* our Miſter Pitt.

                                        without

without any farther accident, either from Cupid or any other markſman, found himſelf at his lodgings in Suffolk Street, near the Middleſex Hoſpital.

CHAP.

CHAP. II.

═══════

Yet when thy *wit* to my enraptur'd eyes,
In all its blazes of bright glory rife :
When with enchanting, novelty you charm,
With *error* pleafe us, and with *truth* alarm;
With awe and wonder I obferve thy plan,
And own that Freedom was not made for Man.

═══════

" BIRDS and beafts have all of them
a method *whereby* to comprehend the mu-
tual fympathy of amorous emotion,
fomehow—But even kings* and princes
of

* Not all kings and princes; for the kings of
Congo and Dahemy, nations of celebrity in Africa, are
barbarous

of the human race are obliged to call in the affiftance of fcholarfhip in fome degree; which is *fo comical*, in order to know the tongue, and dialect, and con-ceits, look you, and notions, and the like (as my countryman Fluellen would fay), of the Fair, whom they would ad-drefs, before they can woo her.

" Now it has always ftruck me, that is. to be lamented, confidering the admi-rably brilliant things which our princes and kings, *in good time*, would fay of their own accord in their native tongues, as our Princes of Wales ufed to do before the time of Edward the

barbarous enough to elect *their* wives from among their own fubjects; whereas, if they fent for them, as ours do, beyond fea, they muft be fure to acquire the *fcholarfhip* in queftion.

Firft,

first, *as I remember.*—And though Balzac terms the studies of foreign languages, the heavy luggage of antiquity, and Locke advises us to fill the mind with reflections; yet I still think the art of raising asparagus, as I saw it practised in 1788*, by one Pierre Le Choux, a gardener near Passy, a village in the vicinity of Paris, is preferable to the common mode adopted in our gardens: but Shakespeare, when he speaks of Biron, in Love's Labour Lost, describes a truly fascinating converser: and the consummate idler, who is determined to make too frequent a use of the favourite figure Aphænesis, may amuse himself by figura-

* Just on the eve of the dreadful revolution. It is a fact, that not a single sprout of this useful diuretic vegetable has since grown in that polluted atmosphere.

tive

tive expreſſions, as I once ſaw in the
great deſort, an Arab called " Mahyla
Aſhog."

So ſpoke a lady at Mrs. Blandford's
converſazione—A lady whoſe general
knowledge does honour to human nature and to her ſex, and, above all, to
the mountains where ſhe was fed by
the nine Muſes (whoſe names ſhe would
tell in a moment, but which I cannot
ſtay to recollect, for my heroine waits
for me)—which Muſes undoubtedly nou-
riſhed her with eclogue-iac, milk mingled
with Hyblean honey. So ſpoke ſhe—
and the learned, the lively, the acute
all liſtened, for *her* converſe was indeed
faſcinating; but at the moment ſhe
named Mahyla Aſhog, Azemia ſtarted
up, caught her hands, and burſt into tears.

" What

" What is the matter, my dear?"
said Mrs. Blandford, alarmed.

" Oh! Madam," cried Azemia in
speechlefs agony—" that Afhog!—he was
a fervant of my father's, and I have
heard my grandmother fay"——" And
what then?" faid Mr. Gallftone, an old
gentleman, who had not yet fpoken.—
" Come, come, my pretty dear, let us
not hear tales of thy grandmother.—
Madam," refumed he, turning fternly
towards Mrs. Blandford, " this young
thing's head is filled with agglomerated
carnofities, generated by novels and romances.—Let her get a good cookery
book if fhe *will* read, and learn how
to make the moft proportionate pud-
dings, and to boil them with the moft
attention to the adhefive qualities of the
oviparous

oviparous and lacteal ingredients. "Sir,"
continued he, addreffing himfelf to Sir
Baptift Bamboozle, who fat by, " Sir,
great abilities are not requifite for cooks,
yet man has been juftly defined as a
cooking animal.—I think Mrs. Glaffe
the firft woman among them; imagination is not required in any part of the
culinary fcience—yet Hannah had great
imagination.   Sir, when I was at Pem-
broke College, I tafted a pot of mar-
malade of her manufacture, and its con-
fiftence and fuavity fet her very high
in my opinion."

To this all the company affented; but
poor Azemia, who underftood not one
word of it, felt extremely diftreffed: fhe
would have given worlds, had fhe poffeffed them, to have fpoken to Mrs.

Albuzzi, the lady who had named (as having feen) this Mahyla Afhog. But while Mr. Gallftone ftaid there was no paufe in the converfation—loud, fonorous, and fententious, all he faid was attended to with eagernefs, and affented to with complacency. At length, having a dofe of rhubarb and jalap to take that night, of which he failed not to inform Mrs. Albuzzi, he ftalked away, and the converfation became more general.

While Dr. Profe was telling a very long ftory about Lord and Lady Laudanum, Azemia approached Mrs. Albuzzi, and, trembling as before the very meridian fun of female information, ventured to afk her to give fome farther anecdotes of Afhog.

" Oh,"

" Oh," cried the lady, " all I faid was merely *typical:* in fact, though I might have feen this perfon, and my imagination is fo lively that I almoft could fancy I did—as Louis the Ninth, you remember, faid to his Almoner— while, in our days, liberty claims a more pofitive fignification, and feems to imply an original grant, a femi-barba- rous, femi-focial ftate, like that of the Tartar nations, who live by rapine and fubfift in wandering hordes, " their hand againft every man, and every man's hand againft them," as was *pro- mifed*, you know, my dear, to your pro- genitor Ifhmael."

Azemia, now totally difcouraged. was going to the other end of the room, leaving this very erudite lady to con

tinue her admirable, though somewhat
defultory animadverfions in men and
things; when she was arrefted in her
courfe by a group of gentlemen and ladies furrounding a languifhing fair one,
who with head reclined, and doing *her
poffible* to raife a blufh—fat, or rather
leaned, on a fopha in a moft becoming
attitude, and looked down, as, in com-
pliance with the entreaties of her friends,
fhe repeated flow, yet fweet, in a *pen-
five* voice, the following

ELEGIAC SONNET

TO A MOPSTICK.

Straight remnant, of the fpiry birchen bough,
  That o'er the ftreamlet wont perchance to quake
  Thy many twinkling leaves, and, bending low,
  Beheld thy white rind dancing on the lake—

How

How doth thy prefent ftate, poor ftick! awake
  My pathos—for, alas!' even ftript as thou
May be my beating breaft, if e'er forfake
  Philifto this poor heart; and break his vow.

So mufing on I fare, with many a figh,
  And meditating then on times long paft.
To thee, lorn pole! I look with tearful eye,
  As all befide the floor-foil'd pail thou'rt caft,
And my fad thoughts, while I behold thee twirl'd,
Turn on the twiftings of this troublous world *.

While thefe things were paffing in
Margaret - Street, Cavendifh - Square,
where Mrs. Blandford had taken a
houfe for three months, Mr. Sheeppen
little thought how near fhe was to him;
but, indeed, had he been aware of it,

* The reader of tafte cannot but recollect the
very moral and affecting meditation on a broom-
ftick, which perhaps fuggefted this idea to the *fair
author.*

as he was now in search of preferment,
he muſt have checked the ebullitions
of his paſſion, as Mrs. Albuzzi * would
ſay, "*ſomehow*;" for a Clergyman of
the Church of England to marry a
Mahomedan, would be "*ſo comical*, I
think;" for (would ſhe probably add),
"cranes and wild geeſe obey a leader,
and reject not ſubordination, which is
paid to *him* who has the longeſt ge-
nealogy †."

* Let not faſtidious critics object to this ſecond
mention of Mrs. Albuzzi. There is in her manner
and her writings a continual corruſcation of catch-
ing lights, which irradiate every prominent point of
intellect, and ſuddenly enable us to ſeize on a chain,
a link, a concatenation of ideas, which we never
ſhould perceive if left to ourſelves.

† Vide Britiſh Synonymy, and other admirable
works.

CHAP.

CHAP. III.

━━━━━

Laugh then at any but at fools or foes,
Thefe you may anger, but you mend not thofe:
Laugh at *your friends*; and if your friends are fore,
So much the better—you may laugh the more.

POPE.

━━━━━

AZEMIA, now every day improving, became infinitely dear to Mrs. Bland-ford. There was to the obferving and reflecting mind of that excellent lady fomething particularly interefting in marking the development of the human intellect, which, till its feventeenth fum-

C 4 mer,

mer, had been in a ftate of infantine
ignorance, and on which the light of
knowledge had burft at once.

Infenfibly the attention fhewn to her
fair protegée induced Mrs. Blandford,
though on very different motives from
thofe which had actuated Mifs Ironfide,
to conquer that diflike to public places,
and more general fociety, which had
originated in difappointment and forrow.
Azemia foon became an object of admiration, as the beautiful Turkifh girl;
and on her account, rather than on that
of her own fuperior intelligence, Mrs.
Blandford found her company fought
by almoft all the literary, and fome few
of the fafhionable world.

Among

Among thofe who moft earneftly foli-
cited her acquaintance was Mrs. Quackly,
the widow of an eminent phyfician, who
lived on a very handfome jointure in a
very handfome houfe in Soho Square,
where fhe made a point of receiving all
thofe who were eminent in the world,
whether for literary acquirements or
any other notoriety.   Here the actor
had an opportunity of ftudying his
author—and the mufical performer affociated with the affluent amateur—the
mineralogift and the botanift might
compare their difcoveries; and the pro-
jector explain his fchemes for the benefit
of the world, to the idle man of fafhion
(who was received only becaufe his *name*
was flattering to the vanity of Mrs.
Quackly), and who cared not if that

C 5   world

world held nothing but the objects immediately gratifying to himself.

Here, with an infinite variety of odd personages, were some who seemed fallen among them, hardly knowing how, by a strange perverseness of destiny; and of these *Mr. Hillary* was soon distinguished by Mrs. Blandford. His person was (though large, and rather what is called heavy) remarkably handsome: he had a countenance so attractive, and a voice and manner so fascinating, to those whom he thought it worth his while to please, that it was impossible to be on one's guard against the seduction of his conversation. Mrs. Blandford was the first to be sensible of its charm: there was a sort of reluctant gaiety about him which seemed to be the effect of philosophy combating disappointment,

appointment, that fuited her feelings particularly; and after meeting him frequently at Mrs. Quackly's, fhe had given him a general invitation to her own houfe, where he often vifited, paying her much of that attention which is at any age flattering, and often fhewing her in confidence fpecimens of thofe poetical talents which began to make fome noife in *the world*.

He was one day prefent when Mrs. Albuzzi was difcourfing on the various meanings of the words folly, fatuity, ideotifm; and faying, that the flexibility of temper, which is ufually called weaknefs, may be driven very eafily to ideotifm : " As," faid the *lively lady*, " I once faw a rich trader prefent a conjuring chemift with a hundred pounds,

C 6   only

only for telling him, that if he would grind his cochineal finer, it would go farther; and a lad, paſt fifteen years old, perſuaded to *burn his fiddle*, be-cauſe," ſaid his playmates, "there is a new diſcovery now, that fiddle-aſhes ſell for a crown an ounce—as there is nothing elſe found out ſo certain a cure for the dropſy. We call this," con-tinued ſhe, "the power of making *fools* of the *people*; and truly do we call it ſo, when mankind are willing to be duped between *deluſion* and *colluſion* ſo far, that they are contented to bury themſelves chin deep in earth . . . . . ."

"Enough, enough, dear Madam," interrupted Mr. Hillary, "you ſay very juſtly; but never, oh! never con-fine your remarks in this manner to *re-tail*

tail inftances, when you may give a wholefale and fublime example of a whole nation. We fee before our eyes a wife and provident people made fuch fools of by this *delufion* and *collufion*, that they have burnt their fiddle, fiddle-ftick, cafe, and all, and are contented to bury themfelves chin deep in debt, from which it is impoffible they can ever emerge—at the fuggeftion of a State Charlatan, who, though regularly bred, and adhering to what is falfely called regular practice, has fo miftaken the *cafe*, that by dabbling in preventives, for which there was no occafion, he has brought on conftipations and ruptures that muft utterly deftroy the conftitution."

The lady's eyes flafhed fire as indig- nantly fhe looked at her old acquaint- ance:

ance': fcorn and anger mingled on her brow, while fhe exclaimed, "And it is thus, *in good time*, that perfons who have degraded and debafed themfelves by their profligacy, and diffipated their fortunes, have recourfe to *levelling* fchemes, *I think*; fo that *their* apoftacy really *frights* one. *Such* a man we all agree to loath, *I believe*, and, with one confent, deteft his conduct, while we abhor his principles."

Mrs. Blandford, who had no idea of the violent party paffions that boiled in the bofom of Mrs. Albuzzi, faw her with fo much diflike thus give way to them, that fhe was very glad when fhe rofe and flounced away; while the gentlemanly calmnefs of Mr. Hillary interefted her ftill more in his favour.

He

He feemed unwilling to dwell on the
foibles of Mrs. Albuzzi, while he fpoke
highly of her abilities; "which really,"
faid he, " are very uncommon, though
rendered fometimes difadvantageous, and
even ridiculous, by vanity and affectation. But when we remember how *few*
of the people who talk about knowledge
know any thing, let us allow this extraordinary woman to infult us a little with
her violent pretenfions. Think, my
dear Madam, how much more general
her knowledge is, and how much more
cultivation her mind has received, than
the men who pafs for fcholars, or fine
writers. She would make, for example,
much better verfes than the Duke, poor
man! who has been flattered into fancying it is neceffary for Mæcenas to fhew
he can practife the art he patronifes;

and

and so makes charades, and writes pro-
logues without even the least ray of
poetry, and with almost as little common
sense. And then there's Blow-up, the
ci-devant dealer in combustibles, who
has for these twenty or thirty years fatigued the ears of play-going people
with his miserable, vulgar, and senseless
flippancies, by way of epilogues, which
he really thinks are superior to those of
Garrick and Sheridan, and loves to an-
nounce to the public, as ' coming from
his pen,' at the earnest entreaty of the
author of the comedy. Then there is
poor Jerrygum, a sentimental writer,
who pipes out most pathetic pieces of
imaginary misery, and sings them to his
own harp, for all the world like Scrib-
lerus, when he incontinently snatched
his *little Lyra,* and in extreme dishabille
                                        went

went forth into the balcony to ſtill the
indecent contention of two Dames de
la Halle of thoſe days, who were ſcold-
ing in the ſtreet :—only inſtead of being
ſans culottes, or *ſans* any other appen-
dage of a Catholic Chriſtian, he ſits
with all imaginable pathos in a pair of
inexpreſſibles ' *couleur de roſe.*' Then
only recollect our acquaintance Fitz-
Jumbling, who has written in verſe a
folio hiſtory of Rome, ſomething in this
ſtyle :

Reader! in this ſhort ſketch 'twould not beſeem us
To ſay too much of Romulus or Remus ;
Nor to extend the long hiſtoric page,
With telling of their birth and parentage ;
Or how from wolves they got their education,
Which made them founders of the Roman nation.

" My

" My good friend," exclaimed Mrs.
Blandford, " tell me, I befeech you,.
what could induce you to repeat fuch
ftuff?"

" Nay," anfwered Mr. Hillary, "let
me rather afk what could induce any
man to write fuch."—And again,

" Next let me fing of Numa, called Pompilius;
Who, like our own good King—was very bilious;.
Yet, we muft own, did not amifs behave—
His minifter, a lady in a cave,
Who taught him to arrange his ftate affairs
Better than thofe that creep up the back * ftairs.

" Then what do you think of the fwarm
of ephemeron writers, who, though a

* Vide Junius, &c.

little

little crufhed and chilled by the ridicule
that has been thrown on them, now and
then venture forth on trembling tender
wing—to fing of hermits living in rocks,
nobody knows where or why; who tell
ftories, and give advice to damfels,
coming from nobody knows whence,
nobody knows for what; or things be-
ginning with

    All in a caftle on a hill,
      A baron did abide;
    And there, alas! againft her will,
      Young Emma was his bride.'

And fuch ftuff about Sir Ederhead,
and Sir Gawine, which they fancy are
old Englifh ftories, or at leaft very like
them."

              " Nay,

" Nay, now," cried Mrs. Blandford, " you are a great deal too fevere.
Think, my good friend, that there are
innumerable young and fimple folk who
love poefy, but who cannot relifh any
thing they are obliged to read twice
over; and that as there is light fummer-
reading for them in the way of novels
and tender tales, fo there is a demand
for fuch eafily-digefted pieces of poetry
as may not overload their delicate in-
telle&s. For my part, I own I am ftill
child enough, or woman enough if you
will, to like fome eafy verfe that fooths
my ear, without giving me much trou-
ble to think whether it be fenfe or no
—one hears *fo* much very good fenfe
that is *fo* tirefome!"

" Mrs.

" Mrs. Albuzzi herself," replied Hillary, " could not have given us a more feminine aphorifm, for the fake of being contradicted. I know you have a better tafte. For example, you are delighted with fome of the leffer poems—where he forgets his fatirical talents, and fheaths his claws—of a certain wicked bard yclept Peter Pindar?"

" Undoubtedly."

" The next time I have the honour of waiting on you I will bring you a flight thing of that fort, written by a friend of mine."

" Pray do," faid Mrs. Blandford; " and in the mean time, if incomprehenfible fublimity, and wild extravagance of

passion,

passion, be your delight, I am sure you
will be in raptures with an Ode, which
I made Azemia cut out this morning
from a newspaper. Perhaps you may
know," added she, casting a sly look at
Mr. Hillary, " the fair authoress, as
well as the dangerous *votary of Apollo*,
to whom it is obliquely addressed,
though called an

ODE TO SENTIMENT.

What art thou, Sentiment, unkind,
That thus within the ruby-tinctured wave
Of lovers' hearts dost love to lave
Thy fangs, that rend the poet's trembling mind
With rapturous, oh! and danger-breathing thrills?
Dwell'st thou on rugged rocks, or high-topp'd hills,
Or art thou to the verdant vales confin'd?
I see thee floating o'er the primrose ground,
Thy brows with garlands of mimosa bound

And

And myrtle-mingling leaves!

Quivering at thy approach, my tear-ftain'd-lids

Are *oped*, as cruel genius bids,

And quick my palpitating bofom heaves!

My fenfes trill!

By mazy rill *,

That feems all form'd of lovers' tears,

The poet of the living lyre appears!

He ftrikes with dulcet hand the chords,

Singing fighs and wounding words;

And fcatters from his pictur'd harp

Spiry † flames and arrows fharp.

Above, below,

They feem to go;

Where threaded finews feem to ftart,

Charged with each—a lover's heart!

---

* Nothing can be more truly appropriate, or more affectingly beautiful, than the image of a rivulet of lovers' tears. How unlike the puerile and profaic images of moft modern poetry!

† The lovers of poetry will inftantly recollect this *daring imitation*, and certainly *improvement* on the fublimity of Gray.

And

And deeply drink my heart's beſt—Oh!
His beamy eyes of ſky-ey blue,
Like ſapphires in their caves of moſſy hue,
Or vernal hyacynths of azure true,
Baptiz'd by Zephyr's hands in flower-extracted dew.
He comes!—Oh! ſilence with thy ermine glove,
Huſh every ſound—but that of him I love;
With ſandals of the thiſtle's * crown,
That feathery floats along the down,
Ye balmy-breathing breezes, move †,

---

* The idea of ſandals for ſilence, formed of the
down of the thiſtle, has in it an originality—a tenderneſs which I never expect to ſee equalled. Cobweb contemplation only emulates this intereſting
image. Methinks I ſee Contemplation thus veiled,
and the ſpiders reſpecting her ſolemn muſing. Then
the tranſition to the luxurious *lyre*, over which *tender wiſhes* are *enwreathed with new-blown roſes*,
gives an image to the mind which it parts with reluctantly.

† Ye balmy winds, *beneath* my *body blow.*

This line is reckoned the moſt beautiful of Pope's:
in my opinion this of Matilda's equals it.

Huſh

Hush every found but *his voice* whom I love,

And oh! be *cobweb Contemplation* wove

O'er his luxurious lyre,

To notes of soft desire,

That never tire!

Be wreaths of tender thoughts and wandering
      wishes thrown,

Mix'd with unfaded roses newly blown!

His trembling ardors he infuses,

Extract from the melting muses;

And softer far,

Than from the reed-woven jar

Florentine oil in pearly-dropping oozes.

Oh! his wild notes entrance my soul,

Yet ah! my transports to controul,

* Iron Remembrance comes; and copper Care,

                      And

---

* Iron Remembrance, is fine: it conveys ideas
of " the iron that entereth the soul," but which the
soul devours in silence; while copper *Care* makes us
at once see something avowed and before the world,
as family cares ought to be. Then *steely* Sorrow suc-
ceeds; *sharp*, yet salutary, and the epithet is doubly

           appropriate :

And Sorrow's steely form, *upon my soul*,

Rouses the *red Remorse*;

Ah! cruel curse

My passion fades,

Duty pervades

My every sense; my bosom's Lord appears *,

Prudence *nears*,

† Eyes and ears,

Your bosom's Lord obey!

Hush'd be your murmurs, heart too tender!

Thou to luxuriant Love must *not* surrender—

---

appropriate : while *red* Remorse finishes the beautiful picture. The reader sees at once that Remorse could not possibly be of any other colour.

* The tender Dame to meet her Lord prepares,
  And Strephon, sighing, slips down the back stairs.

These lines, perhaps, of Lady Mary Wortley Montague, might have occurred to the fair authoress (where she speaks so feelingly of her bosom's Lord), as well as to the *Bard* she addresses.

† There is both moral and pathos in the fair Lyrist's commanding her eyes and ears to obey in future *her bosom's Lord*—who, it is to be hoped, will henceforward "sit lightly on his throne," as our immortal poet has it.

Let

Let Della Crufca thee feduce no more;
But to thy conjugal affection true,
Fly for ever from the view
Of eyes, like *spring-born* Periwinkle's, blue * !
They fade like ftars away;
While I, deep fighing, fay,
What is pleafure, what is May?
Love o'er my couch has ftrewn each fweet,
Love has figh'd, trembling at my feet:
He has indeed,
But o'er the mead
He flies; and Senfibility doth linger †
Only with cruel, quivering finger,
To fay—Henceforth Matilda fhuns
Crufca, and all his wildernefs of funs.

* The *novelty* of comparing blue eyes to the fpring-born Periwinkle, muft, as well as its fimplicity, charm every true lover of the mufes.

† Senfibility lingering to direct the poetefs to fhun the wildernefs of funs, is fingularly happy. It appears by fome other verfes in the delectable newfpaper correfpondence, that, in obedience to Senfibility, fhe took fhelter in *Young Grove's fhade.*

D 2   Mrs.

Mrs. Blandford now ceafed reading—when, to her utter aftonifhment, Mr. Hillary, without the leaft apparent caufe, or provocation, took up his hat, and, glancing his eyes at Azemia with an expreffion nobody underftood, went down ftairs, and out of the houfe, without fpeaking one word.

CHAP.

CHAP. III.

The droning fages drop the drowfy ftrain,
Then think, and fpeak, and fpeak and think again.

COWPER.

BEFORE Mrs. Blandford had recovered of her furprife, Dr. Profe entered—though it was rather at an unufual
hour, and all the reft of the company
had departed.

"How are you, my dear Madam?"
faid the Doctor, in his ufual lively way.

"I am pretty well, Doctor, I thank
you," anfwered Mrs. Blandford.

D 3   "And

" And you, my sweet young lady," added Dr. Prose, turning to Azemia, " how do you find yourself this evening?"

Azemia answered, that she was well.

" We have been a little surprised, though, my dear Sir," cried Mrs. Blandford.

" Pray, my good Madam, with what?" enquired the Doctor.

" With Mr. Hillary," said Mrs. Blandford.

" He *is* apt," answered the Doctor, looking significantly under his brows, " to surprise people."

" So I have often heard; but I cannot say I ever saw any symptoms of it before."

" Lady Canter knows otherwise," said he.

" So

" So I have heard," replied Mrs. Blandford.

" He is a very odd man," obferved the Doctor.

" But can be very agreeable if he pleafes," anfwered fhe.

" I never happened to meet him in one of his agreeable moods, I fuppofe," faid the Doctor.

" Poffibly not," faid Mrs. Blandford ; " but I affure you, my dear Doctor, if you had happened to have come in this evening while Mrs. Albuzzi was here . . . . "

" I never do," interrupted the Doctor, " come knowingly to any place where fhe is likely to be found."

" Indeed !" exclaimed the lady.

" Indeed," replied the Doctor.

" I wonder at that, though, my good Sir; for I fhould imagine, that from

D 4　　　　your

your having vifited the fame countries, and being both literary, you muft have a number of ideas in common, that . . ."

" I hope not," anfwered Doctor Profe, " for I am fure I fhould fay nothing about my ideas if they had any fimilitude to hers; and befides, my dear Madam, with fuch volubility of fpeech as that woman has, what chance in the world fhould I have of being heard?"

" Of *finifhing* a ftory, if you were lucky enough to *begin* it, to be fure, dear Doctor, you would have but little chance; but then, perhaps . . . . ."

Nobody can tell how long this dialogue, with fo fprightly a companion as the Doctor, might have continued, if a violent thundering at the door had not ftartled them both, and a woman

of

of fashion, but lately known to Mrs. Blandford, but an old acquaintance of Dr. Prose's, had not hastened into the room.

"I am come," said Lady Clara Clangor, "to take my leave of you, Mrs. Blandford. And, dear Doctor Prose, what commands have you for Italy? I am going directly—How delightful—is it not? There is nothing I *do* so abhor, as this England of ours. Dandy is gone on before us—You know Dandy—every body knows him. — Is not he an entertaining creature? We are to overtake him at Hamburgh—the dear wretch is to wait for us. Oh! my God—*il me tarde bien*, not to have set out already. Well, but, my dear Doctor Prose, tell me, what do you think of

D 5   public

public affairs? Do you know, some
horrid fellows have been telling me that
the odious filthy wretches will get the
better at laſt!—Oh! my God, if they
ſhould—but 'tis impoſſible.—What ſhall
we be about if they do?—Oh! my good
Proſe, how *could* you ever ſpeak in their
favour? — Do you know, it was vaſtly
ridiculous; and you have no idea how
every creature, whoſe opinion is worth
having, hates a demmy, as we call them.
But tell me, Doctor, what do you think
of things?"

"My dear Lady Clara," began the
Doctor (ſlowly and ſolemnly he ſpoke),
"my dear Lady, there are people whom
people of rank love to have conſtantly
with them, for the purpoſe of applaud-
ing whatever they do or ſay; whoſe
buſineſs it is to prevent diſagreeable
                                    truths

truths from reaching the ears of their patrons, and contribute to make them as vain, weak, ignorant, and capricious, as they themselves are abject, selfish, and parasitical. — Now, my excellent lady, you must allow . . . . . ."

" Oh! my God, Doctor!" exclaimed the Lady, " I will allow any thing upon earth rather than that you should make me a long speech. I dare say your opinions are delightful, only that it will take so much time to hear them, that it is quite impossible for me to stay—for I am going to Lady Mary Macmidling's assembly, and from thence to the Duchess's—and then Scarabée and Squirl, and Jack Swindurn, go home to supper with me.— By the bye, Jack is at this moment waiting for me in the coach; and so, my dear Doctor, to shew you I don't mean

to favage you, and how vaftly delightful I think your converfation, I will
take you with me if you are going towards St. James's."

The Doctor, whether in hopes of ob-
taining an opportunity of concluding the
oration, or for fome other reafon, ac-
cepted this gracious invitation; and
Azemia was delighted to find herfelf
quietly at fupper with her benefactrefs.

"Well, my love," faid Mrs. Blandford, "and what do you t nk of our
vifitors of this evening?"

"Ah, Madam!" replied Azemia,
timidly, "I am but a very incompetent
judge—but to be ure Doctor Profe..."

"Is not amufing, I allow—but I
affure you he is one of the firft men we
have

have as to information. Then there
was, you know, Mrs. Chiverly, who is
accounted fo accomplifhed a woman,
and is fo well connected; and has a fort
of affociation of people of talents about
her, in what fhe calls ' a little quiet
way.'—I obferved fhe talked to you
fome time."

" Yes," anfwered Azemia, " fhe told
me a vaft deal about her family con-
nections; and how Sifter Such-a-one
lived at a great caftle in Yorkfhire. and
Sifter Such-a-one was married to Sir
Peter Pliable, who had a place at court;
and fhe afked me if I did not think
England a great deal better than my
own country. I told her no; that I
difliked it very much, for, except you,
and one or two other ladies, the women
here

here did nothing but find fault with one
another, and tear each other's characters
to pieces; whereas in my native country
they defired only to amufe each other,
and were happy to fit and embroider, or
fing together. She feemed to fmile at
my fimplicity and ignorance, and told
me it was altogether unbecoming in a
Turk, but that fhe hoped I was by
this time a Chriftian, and I fhould
foon learn better. She added, that
when once it was afcertained to her
(which fhe had yet no opportunity of
afking you), that I was baptized, fhe
would fubfcribe half-a-guinea with all
her heart; and fo would Sifter Such-a-
one, and Sifter Such-a-one, and Mrs.
Such-a-one, and dear good Mrs.
Quibus, the excellent patronefs of all
                                    that

that was good and gentle—all, fhe faid, would fubfcribe to the book fhe fhould open for me."

"To the book!" exclaimed Mrs. Blandford, "what could fhe poffibly mean?"

"Indeed," replied Azemia, "that is more than I know. I did not underftand all fhe faid to me—in truth, but very little of it; but I thought fhe feemed to intend me fome kindnefs that fhe fuppofed I wanted."

"You fhall never want any thing, my dear Azemia," cried Mrs. Blandford, "while I live; and Mrs. Chiverly may fpare herfelf the parade of exercifing benevolence, which is never likely to be put to the trial." She then tenderly embraced her beautiful ward, and wiped away the tears that were in her eyes,

eyes, thinking it uſeleſs to mortify the unconſcious girl, by telling her that Mrs. Chiverly was one of thoſe perſons at once oſtentatious and narrow-minded, who love money ſo extremely, that they dare not uſe it, and yet are fond of appearing full of ſenſibility and charity towards thoſe whom they degrade under pretence of aſſiſting, by repreſenting them as objects of benevolence among their great friends. Of ſuch there are numbers to be met with, who gratify two paltry paſſions at once, and, riſing higher in their own eſtimation by the compact, aſſure themſelves they are the very beſt people in the world, and quite *amiable.*

CHAP.

CHAP. IV.

Like *us* they were defign'd to eat, to drink,
To talk, and (every now and then) to *think.*

CHURCHILL.

"MASTER!" cried Bat Bowling to
Charles Arnold, as they *wound* down
Caſtle-rigg, "I am ſure I ſaw two Ex-
ciſemen of Whitehaven among the trees
there; they know, an pleaſe your
honour, that we are comed from ſea,
and I warrant they will ſtop and ſearch
us; what ſhall I do with the Ingine
ſchawl, and the two Barcelona handker-
chiefs?

chiefs? I lay my life we fhall be put into limbo, and made no more account on than a mufty bifcuit."

The moon (which, in all the moft celebrated novels lately publifhed, fhines every night in the moft accommodating manner in the world) had given this alarming information to honeft Bat, Charles Arnold's fea fervant, while he himfelf had long been fixed in contemplation of that beautiful planet, as it hung in filver radiance over the tall fells among which he was wandering.

" Oh!" beauteous Azemia," cried he, fighing, " where art thou? what has been thy deftiny during the almoft twelve months of our cruel feparation!"

Thus

Thus loft in a reverie, Bat was under the neceffity of fpeaking again.—
" Prithee, mafter," cried he, "don't
get into them there brown ftudies. I
tell you we be fcented by a couple of
damned rafcally Excifemen, or Cuftom-
houfe Officers, or fuch like; and the
upfhot will be fome hell of a job or
another."

Charles Arnold rode on.

The folemn fcene through which he
was travelling reminded him forcibly
of thofe where he had paffed the laft
three months—the image of Azemia following him whitherfoever he went.

" It was thus," faid he, ftill regard-
lefs of his fervant, who every now and
then

then ventured an admonitory fentence;
" it was thus that by thy light, fweet
and mild planet, I found under thy
quiet beams, among the rocks of
Seldzfberg, a fhort refpite from what are
called my duties.—Yes! wild northern
region, where I have in a boat paffed
whole nights in gliding through your
labyrinth of rocks—I have envied the
fifher, who earns his fubfiftence among
them; and I have thought, vain thought!
which it will never be in my power to
realize, how happy I fhould be in one
of the boarded huts that are perched on
thofe fantaftic fummits, if Azemia, my
charming Azemia, was within it. There!
there! would be *my* Paradife!

" Quiet retreats of uncultivated nature,
how diftinctly ye return upon my me-
                                        mory!

mory! Would I could retire for ever to your wild folitudes from fcenes of dirt and darknefs—of obfcenity and ignorance, in which I now pafs the greateft part of my time, for no reafon that can poffibly be given, unlefs it be to enforce, as a mere machine, the operation of the

Ratio ultima Regum;

which decides that men are animals, born only to contrive how to annoy and deftroy each other. How can any thinking being believe it? Yet how many other things do we profefs to believe as abfurd; which fo far from believing, we never think about at all! I remember that, till lately, I fhould have ftared at any man, perhaps have infulted him, who had told me that I was a miferable filly

silly fellow to allow myself to be shut up
in a floating dungeon, sometimes under
the command of a capricious or unfeeling
man, for less money than I could earn with
the saw or the spade, while breathing the
fresh air of Heaven, and gazing on the
green bosom of the earth :—and yet such
is the life to which my mother, I thank
her, has condemned me; and which I
have been taught to think an honourable
profession, and one that will produce a
great quantity of glory to me."

"An please your honour," said Bat,
who could not get the Custom-house
Officers out of his head; "an please
your honour, I've a heard how this here
Gert Britton of ourn is the freeest of all
the countries upon yearth, and that there
is no let or hindrunce to a man's doing
as he wull in no shape whatever.—Now,

thinks

thinks I, ſometimes to myſelf, why how
can that be — when there's ever ſo
much money taken from a man, whether
he likes or no; and then if he does but
go for to buy ever ſo little a matter of
counterband goods, whip! he's in priſon!
Now, for my part, I can't think, as I
ſays to myſelf, where'd be the harm of
our trading with folks of other nations,
without all that there.   I can't ſay as I
likes your forrinners—I knows one Eng-
liſhman, with beef and pudding in his
belly, as the ſong ſays, can beat ten
Frenchmen: and I dares for to ſay they
always will on the ſeas, which is our
own eilemint all the world over.   But
then when it pleaſes his Majeſty, God
bleſs him, to give us peace, why I ſees
no why or wherefore, for not enjoying
all the good things of both countries,
                                              and

and all countries beyond fea; for if they want what we can fpare, why not fend it them, and take in change what they can fpare, and we want, without all this racket of counterband and duties? Now that's my notion of trade, and I do think it would be better.—What cheap brandy we fhould have in that cafe!"

" Your laft argument is a convincing one," replied Charles Arnold, laughing, and roufed from his reverie by this characteriftic remark of his man's; "and in general, friend Bat, thy notions are not bad ones. But, if there were no duties there would be no revenue to pay foldiers, and fuch honeft fellows as we are, who you muft allow *do* alfo deferve to be paid, becaufe foldiers only are not fufficient to defend an ifland, as this is where we live."

" Aye,

" Aye, aye, mafter, that's as true as the day. 'Tis *we* that are all in all to old England; and I'll be bould for to fay, that there's ne'r a true-born Englifhman, gentle or fimple, that would not be free to pay us with a good will."

" I believe it, indeed, my good fellow; and therefore you muft not murmur, you know, at duties, and cuftoms, and taxes, that are applied to fo excellen a purpofe."

" Aye, Sir; but I have heard tell as how there be a power of people, who are neither foldiers nor failors, nor does no yearthly thing for their pay, but ride about in coaches, and dreft in gold-laced cloaths, and have defperate fine

houfes, and all manner of good things
to eat and drink ; and thefe people are
paid, they fay, for all this, by the hard
labour of poor folks that all helps to
contribute rates and taxes; and at the
fame time they defpifes them, and tram-
ples upon them, and calls 'em fwine and
hogs, and the like of that. Now to be
fure, your honour, if fo be as that *is*
the cafe, why one can't but think it a
little hardifh, that fome folks fhould
have a great deal of money paid um for
doing nothing but living on the fruits
of the yearth, while others agin fhould
work early and late to raife thofe very
fruits of the yearth, and yet not be allowed enough to keep body and foul together. I got a book put into my hand
t'other day, which was wrot, I believe,
by fome Juftis of Peace up at London ;
and

and it faid, Sir, as how poor folks had
no bifnefs to think; that it was a bad
thing, and ferved only to make them
lofe their time: but I don't underftand
that—What! has not a poor man got a
foul as well as a rich man?—I am fure
our Chaplain have told me he have often
and often. Well—and if he *has* a foul,
what is a foul but what one thinks
with? And if another, becaufe he is
rich, and I am poor, goes for to take
away my power of thinking, why, what
is it but making me not a man any
longer, but a brute, like unto his horfe,
and his dog, only for the fake of ufing
me worfe than he would ufe them? for,
to fpeak the truth, the horfes and the
dogs of lords and gentry are a great
deal better off than their poor neigh-
bours very often."

E 2　　　　"I did

"I did not think, Bat," said Arnold, "that you had been so able a metaphysician."

"No, Sir," replied Bat, with great simplicity, "I don't pretend for to be able to be a physician—but I can see plain enough, that the reason why that there Justis of Peace, or placeman, up at London, as wrote them there books, would not have poor folks *think*:—it's for fear they should find out there's no occasion for such folks as them; and besides, Sir, let poor folks think ever so much, they would not be discontented if they had enough to have comfortable cloathing and wholesome food, and a house over their heads; for, if they thought ever so long, they would know that it's quite an unpossible thing for all men to

be

be rich and high alike; but some must work more than others, and some must be learned men to govern the others, and direct their work for the best, but not make them slaves; and, therefore, the poor would not be angry at not being rich, since it has pleased God to make different degrees of every thing; only the poor that work for those that have no need to work for themselves, ought to have the common comforts of life, which to be sure, Sir, a poor man cannot get now if he tries ever so."

"You speak like an oracle, Bat; and if I were not as tired as I am I would answer you, and give you my notion of the subjects you have been talking of—though, I assure you, we who by courtesy are called *gentlemen* are very often so

E 3 brought

brought up, that the *quality we think with* is no more exercifed than that of thofe honeft fellows, who are never taught any thing but that they muft labour for a mere exiftence. But I'm glad you have got over your fear of Cuftom-houfe Officers. And now, Bat, do *you* think as hard as you can on your fide, and till we get to the next town, which cannot be far off, I believe, and I will think on mine; and perhaps between us both we may make fome notable difcoveries in politics or philofophy."

" Ah! Sir, Sir," exclaimed Bat, fhaking his head, " I knows what you ftodics—I'm much out in my reckoning if you ben't a thinking of your fweetheart more than of talking politics—or about Philofophers—and fuch;
                              but,

but, howfumdever, Sir, fince you de-
fire me to hold my tongue, to be fure
I knows my duty better than to inter-
rupt you."

The mafter and man were ftill
among the fells; the moon had now
funk behind the moft diftant of their fummits, but her declining light ftill irradiated
the deep blue expanfe, and had given
place to myriads of ftars, on which the
eyes of Arnold were fixed.—The
arch of indiftinct brilliance, called the
milky way, feemed juft above his
head.—" What art thou," faid he,
" thou beauteous path of congregated
fires, about which fo many fables have
been imagined?—What is thy diftance
from this filly world of ours, where we
ridiculoufly think of fo much confe-

E 4   quence

quence our paltry pleafures and puerile pains—this very filly world, which is perhaps of no more relative weight in the great fcheme of the univerfe than one of your fmalleft fpangles of ethereal fire?—And you, ye planets, is this fomething denominated a foul, which my uninformed companion has juft called the power of thinking, attached to this frail feeble body? or has it a diftinct exiftence, which, when the miferable turmoil of this ant-hill I now creep upon fhall be over, will poffefs feparate confcioufnefs, and be in a ftate to inveftigate your orbs, and range among fyftems, of which the wifeft of us now underftand nothing?"

Thus fallen from his aërial journey in that confeffion we are all compelled to make, that we cannot long keep above the atmofphere of this our planet, Arnold returned to the contemplation of what was to him the *moſt celeſtial* among its earthly inhabitants, Azemia.

E 5   CHAP.

CHAP. V.

═══════

Soft tremors, trembling terrors, cyprefs glooms,
Lovers and fpectres wandering in the tombs!

═══════

WHILE Charles Arnold purfues his journey towards London—

Chewing the cud of fweet and bitter fancy,

and encouraging that hope which ftill revives in the youthful bofom, however chilled by fear, or repreffed by difappointment, we will *almoft*, in the words of a noble and elegant fentimental

mental authoreſs *, relate (though it will
form a compariſon, perhaps, but little
to our advantage, when contraſted with
our own plain and homely ſtyle) an incident that happened to Azemia, who
was now once more with her bene-
factreſs in the country, and accom-
panying her on a viſit.   We are
happy that the facts are ſo well aſſi-
milated, that we can avail ourſelves
of words, ſo much more *elegant* than
any *we* could have choſen in the de-
ſcriptive and pathetic united.   We muſt
premiſe, however, that a young Iriſh
nobleman had been *very particular* towards our beauteous heroine for ſome
days; and Azemia, who had found the
image of Charles Arnold return upon
her memory with new attractions among

* The elegant Lady H....

E 6   theſe

thefe fweet folitudes, was uneafy at his notice, and very glad when fhe heard one evening that he was to go the next day. The next day, as he did not ap-pear, fhe concluded he *was* gone, and *tranquillized* her fpirits about it till to-wards evening, when—Lord Scud-about had not been named—a circum-ftance occurred that confirmed Azemia in her hopes that he was no longer a gueft at Luxmore Caftle. This flattering conjecture, in fome meafure, reftored her tranquillity: they were in the li-brary, and a falver of macaroons, queen cakes, and bifcuits, with orgeat and lemonade, was brought round, and found very acceptable. Lady Dorothy Dawdle began to amufe herfelf by looking over fome capital caricatures, though her ladyfhip was rather furprifed

to

to find some of them in such a place,
because they were exaggerated represen-
tations of some very great personages,
in situations highly derogatory to their
exalted dignity and *serene* consequence.
Mrs. Blandford was examining a whole-
length picture of the *late* Empress *of all
the Russias*, which covered one side of
the room : and Azemia, having nothing
to do, looked *fearfully* around it ; for
she conceited that Lord Scudabout,
who (unlike the generality of his countrymen) was of diminutive stature, might
be hid in one of the lower recesses of
the mahogany bookcases, and jump out
upon her all of a sudden : however,
discovering no traces of him, she re-
joiced at *discerning* none, and, advancing
towards a glass door, which was thrown
open to admit the fragrance of various
sweet

fweet flowers that in luxuriant perfume
furrounded it, fhe was ftrongly tempted
to ftray upon the *verdant* lawn.   All was
calm—the breezy air breathed odoriferous gales:—her feet with involuntary
motion led her to a walk, where, as
much as fhe had dared, fhe had thought
of Charles Arnold.   The *meeting* beech
formed a canopy above, the *blufhing*,
rofe, and the *twining* * woodbine, in wild
profufion, bent their blooming branches
to fcatter beneath her fteps their fuave
fcents.   Juft as fhe entered the grove
fhe caft her fine eyes towards the apartment once inhabited by the young

* We need not point out to the tender fufceptibility
of refined *elegance*, how this *meeting, blufhing*, and
twining fcene is calculated to foften the heart of a
juvenile female, indulging reveries on the dear youth
of her bofom.

nobleman

nobleman in queſtion: the pink lute-
ſtring curtains waved through the open
window.——Azemia was a little alarmed,
but ſhe proceeded.

The plaintive *Philomela** had com-
menced her evening melody in dulcet
trills.—With ſlow and penſive air the
beauteous Azemia moved: each ſeat,
each ſhrub, recalled ſome dear idea to
her mind; for here glowed the ama-
ranthus; there was reclined the " love
lies a-bleeding," which particularly affected her; and here bluſhed the *gay*

* Philomela, always ſo much in requeſt with the
poets, has lately been preſſed into the ſervice of the
Noveliſt to *a degree*; certainly beyond what the facts
of natural hiſtory authoriſe: but when the ſun and
moon are alſo in continual requiſition, ſhall not a
bird obey the witchery?

carnation,

carnation, the ruby-tinctured pink, and
the somniferous poppy, emulative of the
evening sky, and sacred to the dull God
of dormitorial and sedative happiness.

Wrapt in this sad but soothing contemplation, as in a pelisse, she advanced
till it grew late, and a wheelbarrow, left
there by the carelessness of the under
gardener, obstructed an opening path
apparently designed to lead to some
place (as most paths do, except in novels); its winding turns serpentined im-
perceptibly up an easy ascent: she was
roused from her reverie by finding herself at the top of the hill, where, contrary to all expectation, she beheld a
mausoleum of *black* marble, which put
her extremely in mind of a mosque or a
minaret in her own country. (The ideas
of

of thefe two things were not very diftinct
in her mind.) She did not greatly enjoy the difcovery, for it was now almoft
dark ; and though the moon could not
choofe but rife on one fide, the fun had
entirely funk on the other.

Azemia, however, entered the gloomy
building—fhe knew not why—(We
know not neither, unlefs, becaufe fhe
was guided by fome *invifible impulfe*;
and becaufe it is now neceffary in novels for all the heroines to go into
black marble maufoleums and grey-
ftone ruins whenever they meet with
them.)—However, Azemia approached;
—the door ftood a-jar: the gloom of
the furrounding evergreens, particularly the cypreffes, caft a folemn fhade
upon the occafion ; and an owl from a
neighbouring

neighbouring ivy bufh hooted audibly,
and cried, " Tee-whit!" which Azemia
had heard from Mrs. Blandford's old
houfekeeper was always a bad fign.
She ftopped—fhe fhuddered—fhe was
infpired with a feeret terror!—fhe felt
herfelf irrefiftibly impelled as by an invifible hand to penetrate this drear
abode. The noife fhe made in entering
alarmed her: the door grated on its
rufty hinges; the owl again cried, "Tee-
whit!"—and the wind howl'd—All
ferved to increafe thefe fepulchral horrors of this lugubrious refidence of
mouldering-mortality.

Azemia trembled, as fearfully, fhe
beheld the dome; for the moon now
opportunely coming from behind a
cloud, threw a feeble light through the

long

long casements of painted glass.   Azemia fancied herself Juliet in the vault
of the Capulets—(for, unlike other fo-
reigners, she understood Shakespeare
to a miracle)—and again she shuddered:
a door was half open on the right hand;
she pushed it gently, and found it led
from the mausoleum into the chapel.
She entered the aisle—something white
appeared at the farther end; the rays of
the moon fell directly upon it, and
it seemed to move.—Suddenly the
great bell in the turret tolled, and
Azemia was overcome with horrible
dread, and unable to retreat.   The
tolling ceased, but she heard the tread
of feet: she became immovable; she
uttered a faint scream—a *form* appeared.—*It* perceived her fears—*it*
flew to support her in *its* arms—it
                                    sunk

funk with her on the black marble pave-
ment (on which her *white* drapery
gracefully floated); and nobody can
tell how this terrific scene might have
ended, if Mrs. Blandford, alarmed at
the abfence of Azemia, had not most
fortunately arrived at that moment in
fearch of her, attended by a footman
with a candle and lantern, who found
Lord Scudabout fupporting Azemia,
yet laughing exceffively at the fear he
had put her into. Mrs. Blandford feverely reproving him, he ran to the
ftables, mounted his horfe, and galloped back to his companions at Lord
Oddberry's, from whom he had fuddenly efcaped to execute this frolic,
as if he had forefeen Azemia's evening excurfion.

Mrs.

Mrs. Blandford foon foothed to peace the agitated bofom of her fair ward; and Lady Dorothy Dawdle, who prefided as miftrefs of this hofpitable manfion, declared that Lord Scudabout fhould never enter it again, and that fhe would the next day go with her ponies to the Marchionefs, his mother, who lived about ten miles off, and complain of the indecorous behaviour he had been guilty of.

CHAP.

CHAP. VI.

———

" Why do the Swinish Multitude repine?"
    Quoth fat, 'Squire Gobble, in full swill and cram.
" Rascals!—do *they* expect like *us* to dine?
    " As to their *wanting*, that is all a sham."—
                    From the Dunaas MS. collection.

———

MRS. Blandford, with her fair *protegée*, now went on a short visit to the house of Lady Dorothy Dawdle's son by her first husband.

It is necessary for *us* to give an account of this gentleman and lady.

Colonel

Colonel Brufque, then, born of a military family, and inheriting a handfome fortune, had been brought up to ferve (as they call it) his country; that is, he had entered at thirteen into the Guards, and had a very military air, a fine round red chubby face, a decifive manner, a great contempt for the people, and a firm perfuafion that a gentleman was an animal, whófe higheft pretenfions ought to be to ftrut about in a red coat, and enforce, if it were neceffary, the orders of his fuperiors. Hè feldom read any thing but the Army Lift, or the Court Calendar, and internally had a great contempt for every fort of knowledge, which was not comprifed in thofe two ufeful publications. But his wife and her mother, Lady Dorothy, were of the order of women of fcience;

ence; and Colonel Brufque, who was
glad of every opportunity of relieving
the infipidity of living alone with the
one, and whofe intereft made it requifite for him to pleafe the other, had
given into their fyftem of collecting occafionally all forts of people; and as
they gave excellent dinners, and lived
at an eafy diftance from town, it is in-
conceivable what a variety of perfons
might be found at their villa, between
Eafter and Whitfuntide efpecially.——
Here then various acquifitions of tafte
and information might be made: here
every branch of knowledge was con-
ftantly progreffive, among profeffors or
proficients in every art or fcience that
gives convenience or lends luftre to
focial life.——Here (to arrange them with
due accuracy) were to be feen,

Aëronauts

Aëronauts and Architects, Actors and Archbishops, Alarmists and Auctioneers, Attorneys; Astronomers and Archdeacons, Accoucheurs and Aides-des-Camp, Antiquarians, and Associators and Agents.

Borough-jobbers, Bishops and Biographers; Booksellers, Botanists, Baronets, and Blacklegs; Barons, Brewers, Bankers, and Butts*.

Critics, Counts, and Calculators; Chymists, Counsellors, Captains (led) and Contractors; Curates (rarely) Clerks, Canal-makers and Ciceroni, Convey-

* A Butt is one of the most necessary animals in a great house. The same useful being, under other names, may be found in other parts of this list.

ancers, Cabinet-makers and Cabinet-
minifters.

Divines (dignified), Doctors, De-
monftrators, Dukes, Duchesses, and
Dancing-mafters, (but no Democrats.)

Engineers, Earls, Effayifts, Elec-
tion-men and Electors, Enfigns, Ency-
clopedifts, Enclofure-fchemers, Electri-
cians, Efquires.

Financiers, Flower-fanciers, Fellows
of the Royal and Antiquarian Societies,
Fidlers, Flute-players and Faro-players.

Germans, Geographers, Genealo-
gifts, Graziers, Gamefters, Generals,
Gazette-writers, and Grooms of the
Stole; Gardeners and Guinea-traders,
Gaugers

Gaugers and Gunpowder-makers, Heralds, Houfebuilders and Hiftrionic Heroes, Hiftorians, and Hautbois-players and Harpers.

Jews, Jewellers, Improvers, Italians, Jerkers*, Jobbers, and Informers.

Knights of the Garter, Bath, Thiftle, and St. Patrick; Knights Banneret, Naval and Civil; and Clerks of the Kitchen and King's Friends.

Lawyers, Loungers, Ladies, Laureats, Liverymen, and Lord Lieutenants and Loan-jobbers.

* A Jerker is fomething under Government; probably a very *ufeful* perfonage with a very large falary.

　　Muficians,

Muſicians, Magnetiſers, Match-makers, Middleſex Juſtices, Maroon-hunters, and Marquiſſes; Metaphyſicians, Methodiſts, and Mineralogiſts; Majors, and Maids of Honour.

Nabobs, News-writers, Novel-makers, Nova-Scotia Baronets, and Neceſſary Women.

Orthographers, Officers, Opticians, Optimiſts, and Old Women.

Pickle-ſellers, Philoſophers, Penſioners, Purſuers of the Picتۇreſque, Players, Prieſts, Peers, Paraſites, Party-pamphleteers, Provoſts, Principals, Picture-dealers, Projectors, Phyſicians, Purveyors, and Poets!

Quacks and Quietiſts.

Reviewers,

Reviewers, *Rat-catchers*, Remembrancers, Recorders, Rhetoriticians, Raja-hunters, and Reevites and Runners (to the Treafury.)

Spies, Solicitors, Salefmen, Statefmen, Secretaries, Serjeants at Law, and Stock-brokers.

Troubadours*, Thunder-makers, Tourists, Theologifts, Trinitarians, and Templars and Toad-eaters.

* Troubadours, Wandering Bards, who, in the days of Chivalry, wandered from caftle to caftle, and were fumptuoufly entertained, while they repaid their good cheer by entertaining the Lord and his guefts with fongs and *ftories*. Something of the fame fort may be perceived now in the retainers of fome great houfes.

Under-

Underwriters, Undertakers*, Underſtrappers, and Under-graduates.

Viſcounts, Viol-de-Gambo Performers, Verdurers, Vintners.

Waiters, Wits, Wanderers, Wonderers, Word-catchers, &c. &c. &c.

To deſcribe half the accumulated talent that was every day collected in revolving groups compoſed of characters ſo various, and generally ſo *uſeful*, would be difficult; I feel, indeed, that it would exceed my powers,

---

* Not buryers of the dead : the gentlemen here meant are deſcribed in Comedies of about ſeventy years ago.

even

even though I fhould have the refolu-
tion to extend this, my firft attempt, till
it fwelled into five very large volumes;
and were I fure that, when I had done,
my gentle readers would have the re-
folution to read them all: I will confine
myfelf, therefore, to a dialogue or two
explanatory and illuftrative.

The Lady of Colonel Brufque was
not only a perfonage of high mental
pretenfions, but alfo of very illuftrious
rank; and fhe never feemed entirely
able to forget that Lady Arfinoe Arrogant had married a Commoner, though
he was a man of family not very much
inferior to her own. The Arrogant
blood, however, (in fpite of the elegant
refinement of her mind, and a *tint* of

Metho-

Methodifm, which teaches perfect humility) continually reminded her, at
the head of this magnificent and well-
furnifhed table, that Lady Arfinoe was
deplacée.

One day (to ufe the ftyle, brief
and fimple, of an admirable novelift,
whom I am proud to imitate), the following converfation took place at it:

The company were Colonel and
Lady Arfinoe Brufque, Lord and Lady
Limberham, Sir Frederick Fanfaron,
Doctor Didapper, a Divine; Mr. Climbup, a young man of great promife in
the Treafury ; Sir Marmaduke Manchet,
formerly a Paftry-cook in the city, remarkable for the moft excellents puffs,
but

but lately knighted on having carried
up an addreſs in favour of this neceſſary
and glorious war; Mr. Muſtyflour, a
Commiſſary of Stores, who had acquired
a princely fortune in its courſe; together with ſome men of inferior note:
Lady Dorothy Dawdle and ſeveral other
ladies, among whom were Mrs. Blandford and Azemia.

Politics are a diſagreeable ſubjeƈt,
only when they may occaſion diſcuſſions
wherein inferior people and *vulgars*,
who may happen to be admitted to the
tables of the Great, may raiſe the indignation of " *les Gens comme il faut,*"
by hazarding their abſurd and ill-found-
ed notions. At this table it was accounted certain that every body thought

F 5   alike,

alike, and that all would join in the juſt and elaborate panegyric which Dr. Didapper began in favour of our heaven born Miniſter; who, as he praiſed the turtle, had not only, he ſaid, by wife and vigorous meaſures, imported a more confiderable quantity of that admirable oviparous *Amphiſbea* than at any former period, but had exported a number of nefarious villains to cultivate the European arts in the Southern hemiſphere, and learn to hunt kangaroos, than any former Premier had ever done. He added, that probably the kangaroo itſelf might ſoon become an article of Britiſh luxury.

" Your obſervation is juſt, Sir," ſaid an eloquent Member of the Iriſh Houſe of

of Commons; " and I am free to con-
fefs, that, whether I look forward to the
paft, or turn my eyes back on the future, I am utterly loft in admiration at
the magnitude.of the indefcribable genius of this great Premier. He em-
braces, Sir, with a keennefs of arm, and
a ftrength of eye that is every way won-
derful, a reach of idea beyond the op-
tics of vulgar nerves ; and 'tis impoffible
to forbear to obferve, that, while he
difcourages all trifling and infignificant
levelling, he is himfelf a leveller upon
a moft grand fcale, for he makes the
rich poor ; and though indeed I have
not heard of his making many poor
rich, yet, fomehow or other, I am per-
fuaded in my own mind, as I will be
glad to explain . . . . . "

F 6   " My

"My dear Mr. *Fitz-Solanum**," said Colonel Brufque, "your faculties of ratiocination are admirable; but allow me, on the firſt bluſh of the buſineſs, to remark that ..... Lady Limberham, you have not taſted this fricandeau—give me leave to recommend it to your Ladyſhip; I aſſure you it is made after a receipt I got at Vienna."

"Colonel!" cried Sir Marmaduke Manchet, who always ſeemed to evade culinary converſation; "Colonel! where do you get your Madeira?—I think it

* Not Solomon, as ſome, through error, might read. Solanum is the Night-ſhade—the Potatoe is of this genus; and Mr. Fitz-Solanum might probably *ſpring* from ſome Mileſian family of great antiquity, cultivators of that admirable and nutritive vegetable.

admirable;

admirable; perhaps the very beſt I have taſted ſince the mayoralty of my friend Sir Anthony Armadillo, who, you know, traded largely to the Weſt Indies, and always ſent *his* Madeira there twice."

"' Faith," cried Mr. *Fitz-Solanum*, " I ſeldom get any good Madeira. I had ſome, it is true, about ſix months ago—the very beſt I ever drank ; but the ſhip it was in was taken by a curſed Republican privateer—the devil fetch thoſe free-booting ſons of b——s!"

" As to what you ſay in regard to the poor," ſaid Mr. Climbup to Mrs. Blandford, who had been talking to him in a low voice, " really, Madam, it ſeems to me as if your exceſſive and acute ſenſibility,

fenfibility, which, pardon me, the ladies
are a *leetle* too apt to indulge, has oc-
cafioned you to fee this matter through
a falfe medium : for, after all, now,
really—what have thefe eternal grum-
blers to complain of ?"

" Of exceffive poverty, Sir."

" My dear, dear Mrs. Blandford—
the poverty of the poor!—to hear a
woman of underftanding talk fo!   Good
Madam, how can you feparate a poor
man from his poverty ?   Thefe hewers
of wood, and drawers of water, would
you have them wear filk and velvet, or
drink Champaigne and Madeira ?"

" By no means," replied Mrs. Blandford, mildly; " but I would have the labourer,

bourer, as was the cafe fince I was old
enough to make obfervations, able to carry fome food befides bread into the field
where he toils all day, which, I believe,
is feldom or never the cafe now. I am
told, Sir, that the poor man, in his daily
work, is barely fupplied with bread;
his family often compelled to live on
bran mixed up with greafe, and their
drink only water. Now, as you, and
every advocate for the prefent order of
things and the worthy gentlemen who
order them, have invariably perfifted
in afferting that England never was fo
profperous as at this moment, notwithftanding the juft and neceffary war, I
wifh to have it explained to *me* (who,
as a woman, cannot be fuppofed, you
know, to be able deeply to make thefe
enquiries), how it happens, that while

the

the rich are better, the poor are worfe
off than they were twenty years fince?
and why, if our trade and manufactures
are fo flourifhing, and our refources
ftill fo immenfe, it happens, that our
gazettes are full of bankrupts, our jails
full of debtors; that our feelings are
continually fhocked by public execu-
tions, and that our poor are literally pe-
rifhing with hunger in their wretched
cottages?   Roulfeau, it is true, fays, that
the poor are the immediate children of
the rich.   He is eccentric and chime-
rical, I know, but the facts I have ftated
I know *are* facts—I do know, for I fee
it every day before my eyes, that the
diftrefs of the middling and lower ranks
has increafed, is increafing, and certainly ought to be diminifhed."

"Impoffible,

" Impoſſible, my good Madam—the thing is impoſſible.—(Give me leave to drink a glaſs of wine with you, Miſs Mincer; which do you chooſe?)—I ſay, Madam, that, in the exiſting circumſtances, it appears clearly to me, who am in the Treaſury, the natural reſort of all thoſe ſort of things——(Lord Limberham, ſhall I ſend you any jelly?— Give me leave to help you, Sir Frederic? —A tartlet, Miſs Hickumbottom?)— ſort of things—happen to know a little of all that, that . . . . on the face of— (a little of that Blanc Mange),—it is impoſſible to arrange things otherwiſe than they are."

" Lord! Mr. Climbup," drawled Lady Arſinoe, " by what chance have you begun ſuch converſation as you have choſen for dinner?

dinner?—For goodnefs' fake, don't make one fick with talking of fuch naufeous fubjects! Sir Frederic Fanfaron, you were at the Opera on Saturday. *Can* you tell me who that *exceſſive* odd-looking perfon was with Lady Aviary?"

"Oh, true! I know perfectly whom your Ladyſhip means, but her defignation is beyond me. The Lady Bobkinfes were quizzing her paſt compute: I believe I aſked Jack Biddycoop, but, 'faith, I've forgot what he faid; I dare fay we ſhall fee her at Lady Buckray's mafquerade. Your Ladyſhip will be there?"

"Yes, I fuppofe, one muſt endure it," replied the Lady with the moſt decided apathy, "for an hour or fo; but I ſhall

I fhall make my efcape as foon as I
can. I fufpect that dear woman, who,
to be fure, has a moft unwearied way of
driving all her friends wild in pure ci-
vility, will have an affemblage of all
the queereft animals fhe can mufter, and
that Noah's ark, or Exeter Change, will
be nothing to her collection of odd fifh
and unheard-of fowl."

Sir Frederic now whifpered the lady,
who nodded, and cried umph; and, as
the deffert was foon after finifhed, and
the ladies had taken their wine,
the party broke up. The next day
Mrs. Blandford left a houfe in which
the fociety fo little fuited her; but was
very much furprifed to receive, on
reaching her own houfe in Hertfordfhire, which was eleven miles diftant
from

from Colonel Brufque's, and about twice
the diftance from Lady Buckray's, a card
of invitation to her Ladyfhip's mafqued
ball for herfelf and Azemia.   With this
lady Mrs. Blandford had been acquainted from her infancy: they were
fchool-fellows, and had lived, for the
firft fifteen years of their lives, much
gether—when one had married an Irifh
Peer, and the other a Country Gentleman.   Their friendfhip now languifhed
on the part of the woman of fafhion,
who ftill, however, nodded and fmiled
whenever fhe faw her old friend, and
occafionally lamented how forry fhe
was that they did not meet more
frequently ; declared how little pleafure
there was in her ftation of life ;
how fatiguing it was to go to Court ;
and how happy fhe fhould be if ever

                                    her

her Lord's avocations permitted them to retire ſnugly into the country to ſocial and domeſtic happineſs, where ſhe could ſee her old friends in a quiet comfortable way.

Mrs. Blandford, to whom neither the moſt brilliant nor the ſnuggeſt of theſe aſſociations could afford any pleaſure, never ſeemed to doubt the ſincerity of theſe profeſſions, becauſe ſhe cared nothing whether they were ſincere or no; nor did ſhe ever appear to reſent an eſtrangement which did not at all affect her. She was, however, little diſpoſed to attend a maſquerade; an entertainment for which, though ſhe did not think it much more dangerous to young people than others, ſhe had no predilection. She therefore ſent an excuſe; but was the

the next day furprifed by a vifit from
Lady Buckray herfelf, who fo earneftly
preffed, and even infifted on Mrs.
Blandford's obliging her, that, rather
than appear to refent her former cool-
nefs, fhe agreed to be prefent with
Azemia at this fête, and that they would
ftay the night; Lady Buckray affuring
her that fhe need not encounter the
fatigue of returning, as there were beds
at her fervice. Mrs. Blandford, however, in affenting, could not but re-
colle&t what had paffed at the table of
Colonel Brufque, nor help fufpe&ing
that fhe was among the odd fifh, and
unheard of fowl, hinted at by Lady
Arfinoe.

CHAP.

CHAP. VII.

———

" I do beguile the thing I am."

SHAKESPEARE.

———

" And painted Flattery hides her serpent train in
flowers."

GRAY.

———

NOVEL-writers are accustomed to amuse their readers with masquerades, as well as with ghosts. Following then one or other of our two most cele-brated writers (Fielding and Madame D'Arblay), I am strongly tempted to

try

try my fkill in the arduous tafk of de-
fcribing, at full length, the adventures
of the mafquerade: but my modefty
conquers my ambition. Repreffed,
therefore, by that humility which I
hope will be deemed graceful by the
beft judges, I will confine myfelf to a
defcription taken from a diurnal print,
the proprietor of which was prefent,
and which is fo admirably done, that I
fhould defpair of making my account,
were I to attempt it, at once fo com-
prehenfive and fo brilliant.—*Allons
donc!*

" On Tuefday laft the grand mafquerade and fête, fo long in prepara-
tion, and fo much the objeᶜt of ex-
peᶜtation in the firft circles, was given
at the Right Honourable the Countefs
of

of B——s——, at her delightful villa of
Laurel Lodge.   The fuper-elegant and
tafteful decorations were highly creditable to the care and contrivance of
Signor Babinetto, who conducted them,
as well as to the exquifite tafte, and
beautiful fancy, of the fair and noble
directrefs of this magnificent entertainment.   The great faloon was hung with
rofe-coloured fatin, feftooned above
with a drapery of filver crape, bordered
with foils of various colours, and knot-
ted up at intervals with wreaths of the
fineft artificial flowers, mingled with
gold and filver taffels.   The leffer faloon was fitted up to reprefent the hall
of Jonquils, as it is defcribed in one of
the fairy tales from the admirable pen
of Madame La Comteffe D'Anois;
but, elegant as it was, the great drawing-

room exceeded it. This fuperb room opens on the fouthern lawn by a pair of very large folding-doors of the fineft crown glafs: the beauty of the internal arrangements of this room may be imagined, by our readers of tafte, when we inform them that, on each fide, were placed reprefentations of various trees, fo admirably done, that they conveyed a complete idea of " the Fathers of the Foreft." In fhort, it admirably prefented the Enchanted Wood of Taffo; and at a given time, when much of the company was collected into that apartment, a mafque reprefenting Rinaldo, a perfon of high diftinction, entered, ftruck thefe maffy repofitories, and, lo! from each ftarted an angelic nymph, who were, we are affured, fixteen of the moft celebrated beauties in fuperior life.

Their

Their lovely hair flowed gracefully on
their shoulders, crowned with myrtle;
their drapery was the lightest and most
transparent: in a word, they were the
forms embodied that had glowed in the
luxurious, the florid imagination of the
Italian poet. These ladies, joined by
an adequate number of the most interesting masques in the room, immediately composed a d ance previously
studied for that purpose, and which was
soon increased, till it struck into a
country dance; and the joyous company danced from the great drawing-
room quite out upon the lawn, on each
side of which there were ranged, pa-
rallel to the artificial trees above-men-
tioned, orange and myrtle, and other
odoriferous exotics—garlands of coloured lamps being suspended from one

G 2

to

to the other. This vista of radiance
was closed by a statue of Minerva,
crowning the bust of our heaven-
born Minister, as the political saviour
of Britain: it was surrounded by *transparent* paintings, or rather deceptions,
of very ingenious contrivance. One
represented Political Rhetoric in the
act of making

The worser seem the better reason;

and the other Prudence, instigated by
Fear, putting a padlock on the lips of
Common Sense; who, not being able to
speak, seemed to express the pain of
this enforced silence by menacing con-
tortions, which the company seemed to
consider as a mighty good joke.

The

The rareſt delicacies of this and every other country were prepared as a rin-freſco, under a ſuperb tent of white tiffany, lined with ſky-coloured ſarcenet, placed near this group of emblematic figures: it conſiſted of ices, jellies, conſerves, fruits of all ſorts and ſeaſons; cold meats of every deſcription; poultry and game:——earth, air, and water had been ranſacked to contribute to this moſt elegant *fête!*——After the *goûté*, a band of muſic was called from the adjacent woods, who played the air dear to the heart of every true Briton,

" God ſave the King,"

and a full chorus repeated it three times three. After which, the whole concluded by an aſs-race: the laſt who came in to poſſeſs, as prize, a cap, with a figure of

G 3   *Moria*

Moria upon it in coloured foil, which
was won, with eafe, by the Honourable
Thomas Titmoufe.   After another flight
refrefhment with liqueurs, the company
departed highly gratified by their entertainment, and the fuavity and complacency of their amiable hoftefs.

A masquerade generally produces a
great variety of adventures, and almoft
as generally an elopement, or an *enleve-
ment* of the heroine: in the prefent inftance, however, I choofe it fhould be
otherwife.   Nothing is fo enchanting
as novelty—from its name it muft, of
courfe, be the foul of a novel; and
therefore to give this, at leaft in one
inftance, I beg leave to relate, that
Azemia, though dazzled by the fplen-
dours of " the furrounding fcenery,"
was

was rather diftreffed by the figures that peopled it. The hideous mafks that on every fide met her eyes, on which were all the deformities that could render dif-gufting

" The human face divine."

fometimes aftonifhed, but oftener ter-rified her. From the flippant pertnefs of fome of the women, from the infolent familiarity of many of the men, fhe fhrunk in difmay; and turning from thefe, fhe met only among the very fine people, mawkifh fatiety, or cold indif-ference; for they were of thofe, who, while they languidly attempted to fhew that they were amufed, betrayed the melancholy truth that they were tired to death.

G 4

One figure among this motley group, however, particularly attached himself to her: he was clad in a dreſs that he meant ſhould imitate that of an ancient Britiſh bard; and on his head he wore a wreath of oak, and he had put leaf gold on ſome of the leaves, left it ſhould fail to be conſpicuous. He bore a ſmall harp in his hand, on which he ſometimes ſtruck chords that ſounded to the ear like harmony; at others he played very ill ſome of the vileſt and moſt unmeaning traſh that ever iſſued from the brain of

" Maudlin Poetefs, or rhyming Peer!"

This man choſe to follow Azemia wherever ſhe went with the moſt fulſome flattery, till at length ſhe was compelled

pelled to quit the young ladies, with whofe party fhe had been trying to amufe herfelf, and feek Mrs. Bland-ford, whom fhe found fitting alone in an alcove of the garden, fome-what remote from the company ; where, though fhe forbore to fay fo when our heroine joined her, fhe had been con-templating the ftrange and capricious difpofition of the things of this world.— " Here," faid fhe, " are a fet of people got together to try to be happy—the leaft nicely dreffed, the leaft expenfive among them, probably pays for his or her night's diverfion twice as much as would keep for a week a man, his wife, and three or four children, in the ne-ceffaries of life.—The lady of the houfe, who fo elegantly entertains her guefts, will probably find the amount of her

tafteful

tafteful hofpitality debit her in a fum
that would have been a handfome,
nay, a great portion, a century and a
half ago, for the eldeft daughter of her
illuftrious houfe; and yet all this is in
a country which they fay is ruined, and
which really is fo, if one may judge by
the apparent condition of more than
two thirds of the people. How many
induftrious perfons, who have laboured
all day, fhrink fupperlefs to their hard
beds, trying to forget in fleep the faint-
nefs of hunger! How many mothers by
the light of this clear fummer moon
fhining through their fcanty, and perhaps broken, cafements, gaze on their
fleeping children with aching hearts,
uncertain if, with the coming day, they
fhall be able to find for thefe uncon-
fcious fharers of their poverty that
subfiftence,

subsistence, which half the expendi-
ture of one of these gay individuals that
are now glancing about before me,
would have amply supplied, not for
one only, but for many days!"

Such were the contemplations of Mrs.
Blandford; but such contemplations were
totally unnecessary on the Levant, and
Azemia had not been long enough in
England to have learned to make them,
nor did her protectress wish that she
should.

All Azemia's wishes at present, therefore, went to the shaking off her importunate new acquaintance, who had in-
sisted upon being allowed to be called
her bard; sung songs, such as they
were, in her praise; and quoted com-
G 6   mon-

mon-place speeches with a vehemence
of voice and manner that had very
much diftreffed her.

When they joined Mrs. Blandford,
his adulation took a more quiet and
more fentimental turn : he walked with
her, acquiefced in every thing fhe faid,
praifed her fentiments, and extolled her
tafte to the fkies. At length, he pre-
vailed on the two ladies to fuffer him to
attend them to the fideboard, where in
a manner, *tout patelin,* which, as Mrs.
Blandford did not know the man, fhe
was not upon her guard againft, he
begged leave to toaft with them the
friend moft efteemed by both the ladies. Mrs. Blandford, half laughing
at the obfolete vulgarity of the propofal,
agreed, however, to humour it, for
                                    the

the abfurd *fanfaron* fort of manner of
the bard with his harp amufed her.——
She gave, therefore, a celebrated orator,
in whofe praife the fon of Apollo very
eloquently held forth ; and then turning
to Azemia with an odd fort of fmirk on
his face, he gently entreated her to favour him with hers.

Mrs. Blandford having explained to
her what was defired, becaufe fhe had
only imperfectly comprehended it, Azemia in the fimplicity of her heart, and
becaufe fhe in truth liked nobody better, gave Charles Arnold.

Our bard now affected to be ftruck
with the greateft pleafure and furprife :
he repeated rapturoufly the name of
Charles Arnold, at the fame time de-
claring,

claring, that he was the beloved companion of his childhood (though Azemia, who now saw his face, could not
imagine how that could be), and the
cherished friend of his youth. He then,
soliciting the ladies to sit with him on an
artificial bank, covered with green velvet to imitate moss, under one of the
beautiful orange-trees on the lawn,
spoke thus—having introduced his *eloge*
by an harangue in praise of humanity,
and sensibility:

"My invaluable friend Arnold has
always been the most tender-hearted of
human beings. I have attended to the
dawn of his being—I remember when
we both rode hobby-horses together,
(though I was a little his senior, I still,
as indeed I have always done since,
loved

loved a canter on that amiable contrivance.); I say that in our infantine
sports I watched the progress of the
sacred spring of Pity's heavenly dew,
which has since spouted forth a foun-
tain of living water—(even such as sprang
from the rock at the call of Moses)—and
who, like him, was always so full of
" the milk of human kindness!" Was
a lamb to be domesticated—to him it
was given; and not its own woolly
mama could nurse the firstling better
(except in the article of lacteal nourishment, which was happily supplied by
skim milk.)—Was a calf to be hobbed—
to him, to my beloved Charles, was
delegated the tender task of hobbation;
and through his fists (little fists they
were then) was imbibed the nourishment of the lowing orphan. Io herself

hardly

hardly made a more dulcet nurfe. Was a brood of young turkeys to be reared— it was he—he himfelf, my foft-hearted friend, that gave each of the plaintive neftlings an exhilarating pepper-corn: it was he who fed them with chopped eggs, and mingled clivers with their fnowy curd!

" Was a chicken neglected, pecked, ill-treated by its mother—my dear Charles wrapped it in flannel, put it in a fmall bafket, and endeavoured by fufpenfion near the fire's genial warmth to fupply the animal heat of its unnatural parent!

" Had that parent the pip—he forgot her inhumanity, and thought only of her diftrefs: he opened the oil-containing bag

bag with his beſt knife—he cured, he
releaſed her.

"Never, dear friend! ſhall I forget
his tenderneſs—his ſenſibility towards a
gudgeon—he had caught it. The innocent piſcatory ſufferer looked pi-
teouſly up in his face; ſtruck with the
pathetic appeal, he obſerved to me—
'My Courtney,' ſaid he, 'this fated
fiſh may have friends—may have con-
nections in this limpid ſtream: nay, he
may even have ſome amiable, ſome
ſilver-ſpotted maiden gudgeon waiting
his arrival, under the roots of that willow!—An oyſter, *we know*, may be in
love, and a gudgeon, of courſe liable,
be more diſtractedly enamoured in proportion to his ſuperiority of ſuſcepti-
bility;—but while I expatiate my prey
expires.'

expires.'—So faying, he releafed the
unoffending fifh—it glided away, and
in that moment, what muft have been
his generous feelings? Amiable youth!
my heart glows with participating fympathy—Humanity marked him for her
own, and he has honoured her adop-
tion."

The oddity of this oration extremely
amufed Mrs. Blandford, who was not
without a tafte for humour and fingu-
larity of character. The converfation,
however, of the *foi-difant* bard, (whofe
name, out of mafquerade, was Perkly,)
was of that defcription, which, though it
entertains even by its abfurdity for a
few hours, varies afterwards, and not
unfrequently makes the lifteners repent
the attention they at firft gave, if it

feems

feems to occafion repeated claims for the fame exertion of complaifance.

Mrs. Blandford, therefore, gave no encouragement to Mr. Perkly, when he faid with great apparent delight, that he was now on a fummer tour among his friends, and that he was fo fortunate as to be going the next day the fame way, as that which led towards her refidence in Hertfordfhire, and would fet out at the fame day and fame hour, in order to have the fupreme felicity of efcorting her and Azemia on their way.

The next day came, and a fatigued and heavy-eyed party of the guefts af-fembled at an elegant breakfaft, where, after the delights of the preceding even-ing had been difcuffed, the converfa-tion

tion would have languished, had not
some of the company, and particularly
Mr. Perkly, produced sundry efforts of
their muses in the forms of rebuses and
charades—happy and fortunate re-
sources against those awkward suspen-
sions of ideas which sometimes occur
in the very best society.

To accommodate such of my readers
who may occasionally be bored with the
blank and comfortless sensation of having nothing to say (when they have no
masquerade to talk of and no entertaining
novel, like this, to recommend to their
auditors)—I here set down from memory some of these interesting *jeux
d'esprit.*

CHARADE

CHARADE, BY VISCOUNT ******.

My firſt is rude, ſtormy, and windy,
    My ſecond, ſoft tender and blue :
O Celia ! if you were but kind, eh !
    How bleſt might the whole be with you!

ANOTHER, BY MR. PERKLY,

*More remarkable for the propriety of the ſentiment
than for harmony of numbers.*

My firſt I cannot name to ears polite,
My ſecond was my character laſt night :
When we adopt my whole, and ceaſe to fight,
I hope, with all my heart, things will come right.

An odd-looking man, with a black
cropped head, and rather a ſtern coun‑
tenance, who had long ſat ſilent, and
ſomewhat ſulky, then deſired the atten‑
tion of the company to a new one of his
                                    which,

which, notwithſtanding an angry look
from the lady of the houſe, he produced, and which was to this effeɔt:

> If I *could* do my firſt,
>   I would ſoon from his ſtation
> My ſecond diſplace
>   For the good of the nation
> And then in my tout
>   I would make an oration.

Either the Counteſs was a remarkable
good gueſſer at charades, or had heard
this before. However that was, ſhe
aroſe in apparent diſpleaſure; and ſay-
ing her ponies were waiting to take her
an airing round the park, thoſe who
were returning to their reſpeɔtive homes
that morning took leave, and the company diſperſed.

CHAP.

CHAP. VIII.

━━━━

If every juſt Man, that now pines with want,
Had but a ſeemly and ſufficient ſhare
Of that which lewdly pamper'd luxury
Now heaps upon ſome few with vaſt exceſs!

                              MILTON.

━━━━

MRS. Blandford and Azemia now ſet
forth to return home, not in the carriage of the former, for it had been left
in London to be new lined and painted;
it was an hack poſt-chaiſe that conveyed Azemia and her maternal friend,
while Mr. Perkly, who was, he ſaid,
                              going

going the fame way, ambled by their fide on a pony.

They had proceeded about half way, when the poftillion ftopped fuddenly, and, difmounting in a great hurry, went to the hind wheel of the carriage, and prefently, with marks of concern, in-formed the ladies that the linch pin was loft, and there was danger of their being overturned if they did not get out. Mr. Perkly, riding up at the fame time, defired leave to hand them out into a neighbouring cottage which appeared under a group of tall elms and walnut trees, about fifty paces farther, where the road receded, forming a fort of green, behind which rofe a woody hill. The look of the place was inviting, it would have made a fweet landfcape;

and

and Mrs. Blandford willingly agreed to
fit down on a bench at the door, till
fome remedy could be found for the
defect in the vehicle. They approached; but the fun, as it was now about
two o'clock, was very oppreffive, and
as the trees threw their fhade on the
other fide the hedge, Mrs. Blandford
pulled the ftring of the latch, and, followed by Azemia, entered the cottage.

She was furprifed to fee only a very
old woman, quite paralytic, and very
deaf, who held in her feeble arms a
new-born infant, while a little creature,
not two years old, was hanging on her
gown, and expreffing, as well as it could,
its want of food, which the poor old
woman was apparently preparing for it,
over a few embers, in an earthen pot.

Mrs.

Mrs. Blandford, whose appearance
and questions seemed to make little im-
pression on this half-senseless being,
learned, with some difficulty, that she
was the mother of a poor woman, who
had the day before been delivered of
the little infant, her eighth child: the
father, she said, was out at work four
miles off—the eldest boy only at ser-
vice. The second was gone to tell the
doctor, who lived six miles off, that his
mother was very ill, and to get her
some doctor's stuff: the eldest girl was
sent to beg some linen of a charitable
lady, but she lived at a great house still
farther distant. The second girl was
nursing her mother, and her third and
fourth sisters, who were both sick in the
same room, with what the old woman
termed a *despert* bad faver; and the
mother

mother herfelf, fhe faid, had tafted nothing that day but a little tay; for that,
till James comed back, they had not a
bit of bread in the houfe.

Affected by this account, and the
extreme poverty which every thing
within this abode exhibited, Mrs. Blandford defired to fee the poor woman;
and taking in her arms the new-born
infant, which its infirm grandmother
feemed incapable of carrying fafely, fhe
followed her trembling fteps up a fteep
ftair to a room, where a fpectacle of
ficknefs and want prefented itfelf that
wrung her heart.

The mother, pale and faint for want
of neceffary nourifhment, and on a
wretched bed, was half raifed from it,

H 2   furveying

surveying one of her children, a girl of
five years old, who seemed to be in
extremity; while in a corner of the
room, on a few rags, lay another girl
about seven.   Mrs. Blandford presently
perceived that the complaint of the
children was a low fever, the effect of
bad nourishment; and that the mother,
between the anxiety of her mind and
the weakness of her situation, would too
probably perish.   Her pallid countenance, her sunken eyes and parched lips
were evidences too strong of her suffer-
ings; and Mrs. Blandford, always active
in benevolence, was eager to give this
sad group immediate relief.

This, however, was by no means easy.
This lone cottage was the only one
within three or four miles, and the
nearest

neareft were not likely to fupply any
of the articles neceffary for thefe poor
objects: it was fo far to the town, that
before any meffenger could be fent and
return, the evils fhe wifhed to remove
might become irremediable.   What was
to be done?   In fuch a cafe, all confideration for her perfonal convenience
was forgotten by this excellent woman—
fhe endeavoured to comfort the languid
fufferer with affurances of fpeedy relief;
then, haftening down, fhe went to the
place where Mr. Perkly and her fervant
were affifting the poftillion to remedy the
defect of the wheel, which, it appeared,
was of more ferious confequence than
they had at firft imagined, inafmuch as
the wheel itfelf was broke.   Mrs. Blandford now defired the poftillion to mount

H 3   one

one of the horfes, and haften to a neighbouring town.   The man grumbled, and
demurred.   Mrs. Blandford, however,
infifted; and though Mr. Perkly obferved that it would be better to fend
her own fervant, yet, as he was mounted
on a favourite old horfe, fhe refufed to
alter her intentions, and, after a long
argument, in which Perkly gave his
opinion with more freedom than Mrs.
Blandford thought his acquaintance with
her authorifed, the poftillion departed;
and Perkly, who feemed to think this
delay an inconvenience to himfelf, was
very coolly told by Mrs. Blandford,
who was already tired of his poor attempts at wit, and his hypocritical parade of fentiment, that there was not the
leaft neceffity for her to reftrain him,
                                    and

and that he had much better go his own way, fince it was very uncertain how long fhe might ftay.

Mr. Perkly, who had reafons of his own for wifhing to keep that fhare of Mrs. Blandford's favour which he imagined he had obtained, now began to change his tone; and the good lady, who could not imagine what motive he could have for his uncommon attention, which he paid principally to her (for of Azemia he took little notice), was for once, notwithftanding her natural intelligence, and the judgment fhe had acquired in a long intercourfe with the world, induced to believe that he really found pleafure in her converfation.

Willing,

Willing, therefore, to make it as in-
ftruĉtive as pleafurable, fhe began, as
they all fat together on the bench near
the cottage door, waiting the return of
the poftillion, to enter into a difquifition
on the various conditions of men in a
ftate of civilized fociety. This was begun by Mr. Perkly's faying—" You
feem much interefted, Madam, for thefe
poor people."—" Should I not be def-
titute of feeling, were I otherwife?"
faid Mrs. Blandford. " Can I do otherwife than confider them as beings formed
with the fame feelings, and liable to the
fame neceffities as I am? And can I,
after having been lately in a fcene of fuch
luxurious profufion, help being fhocked
to think, that, while a perfon like our
hoftefs of laft night can, for a few hours
amufement,

amufement, expend a fum that would make many families happy for years, there is, within a few miles of her fplendid abode, a poor induftrious group, a father and mother, an aged grandmother, and fo many children, who are actually liable to perifh for want of the mere neceffaries of exiftence?"

"But, my dear Madam," cried Mr. Perkly, eagerly.

"And, my dear Sir," interrupted Mrs. Blandford, "I know every thing you would fay. The common-place, and, pardon me if I fay, the unfeeling objections that have a thoufand times been made, and a thoufand times incontrovertibly anfwered—I mean to the me-

H 5   lioration

lioration of the condition of the lower
ranks in this country."

"Good God!" exclaimed Mr. Perkly, "is it poffible that a woman of your
fenfe—of your underftanding, can, for a
moment, allow yourfelf to be fo mifled
by the nonfenfical clamour of the multitude, as to imagine that a plan could
ever fucceed that went to univerfal
equalization?"

"No, Sir," faid Mrs. Blandford
coolly, "I do *not* join in that clamour.
I know, and fo does every body of common fenfe, that equality, according to
the fenfe you affect to annex to it,
cannot exift: but there ought to be
equal laws for all men."

"And

" And *are* there not ?" cried Perkly, eagerly. " Is there a country under Heaven where law is-fo equally dealt as it is in ours ? Is there not juftice to be had for every body ?"

" Juftice!" anfwered Mrs. Blandford. " Oh! mockery of terms! You may as well fay to the wretched pauper who befeeches in the ftreet your charity to relieve his hunger—' Friend, why are you hungry ? There is a tavern open on the oppofite fide of the way, where you may eat your fill.'—Would not this be a barbarous infult to the poor men_ dicant's diftrefs ?—Yet it is precifely thus people talk who urge to the op_ preffed in common life the excellence, the equality of the Englifh law.—' It is very excellent, I dare fay,' might the

H 6   fufferer

sufferer reply, ' but I have no means of buying it; for, whatever it can do for me, I muſt pay ſo high, that, if per-adventure I get relieved from the op-preſſion I complain of, I ſhall be as much impoveriſhed as I am now.'—No, never talk, my good Sir, of the equality of our laws, while a Chancery-ſuit is ranked as an evil of as great magnitude as a fire, an inundation, a deſcent of the enemy, or an earthquake; and really as to the ruin they produce, I ſee but little difference—what difference there is, is rather againſt a Chancery-ſuit: the invaſion, inundation, earth-quake, may render a family houſeleſs and deſolate at once; a Chancery-ſuit keeps them in lingering miſery for years, and leaves them beggars at laſt.''

" Well,

" Well, well," said Mr. Perkly, who felt, though he determined not to own it, that he had hitherto the worst of the argument; " well, well, but . . . . that . . . a . . that . . . a . . is not . . . a . . my meaning. No, no—I mean, dear Madam, *that* equality of property, or, as we say, the Agrarian Law, about which so much nonsense has been talked."

" I do not know," answered Mrs. Blandford, " that it might always be such absolute nonsense, however impracticable it is in the present state of society. That it is impracticable, I believe: if any twelve mechanics, for example, of nearly as can be, in such numbers, the same age, intellects, and information, as well as the same bodily powers, were each to have a certain portion of land

assigned

affigned them, with inftruments of huf-
bandry to work, and grain to fow their
fields, you would fee that fome would
be ignorant, fome idle, fome, perhaps,
unfortunate and unfufpecting; fo that,
before two years had paffed, the faga-
cious, the induftrious, the fortunate, the
cunning, would have poffeffed themfelves of their neighbour's property;
and thefe would have two, three, or
more fhares, while the idle and diffipated would be entirely bereft of theirs,
and then, of courfe, there muft be an
end to the equality with which they fet
out."

" Such men then," faid Mr. Perkly,
" would be impoverifhed through their
own folly."

" Moft

" Moft of them, undoubtedly."

" And yet," cried he, exultingly,
" you feel a great deal of pity for the
poor; and feem to think that thofe who
have great affluence are never to enjoy
themfelves in any elegant amufement,
becaufe there may happen to be poor
people in the world?"

" Not fo," replied Mrs. Blandford;
" it would be requiring of human creatures virtuous felf-denial, which I cannot
expeft in civilized, or perhaps any
other fociety. All I mean is, that when
the thinking mind is fhocked by fuch
ftriking difparity as between the fcene
I was in laft night, and what I now
witnefs paffing in this houfe, it is very
apt to advert to the great nations where
                                    fuch

fuch fymptoms were the forerunners of
dreadful convulfions. It is a difeafe
which we know from repeated experience is fatal: I would prevent its being
fo here; I would not have the rich live
much worfe than they do, but I would
have the poor fupported a great deal
better."

"I don't fee that they want any
thing," faid Mr. Perkly, carelefsly, "or
if they do, 'tis only becaufe they are
drunken, or idle."

"Would to God," exclaimed Mrs.
Blandford, "that you, Sir, who have,
as you fay, no wife or family, were
compelled to live, for one month only,
on the fum that, during that fpace, fupplies the labouring owner of this cabin,

his

his wife, mother, and feven or eight
children, with all the means of life!
Believe me, good Sir, you would find
yourfelf moft terribly ftraitened; and
you would then, perhaps, own, that the
poor are not quite fo well off as they
ought to be in a country of whofe pro-
fperity thofe that live on the fat of the
land fo feduloufly endeavour to con-
vince us."

Mr. Perkly ftared, and fhook his ears
at this, as if he was not quite eafy at
hearing even the remoteft hint of fuch
an experiment.

The meffenger foon after returned
with the fupplies directed by the benevolence of Mrs. Blandford, who gave
another

another hour to feeing them difpofed of
for the comfort and relief of the poor
family. She then renewed her journey
with a grumbling poftillion, and one
tired horfe, Mr. Perkly looking fometimes as if he repented of his having
thus volunteered in the fervice of one
whofe feeling, or affectation of feeling,
made his gallantry tedious and troublefome; for, not content with having
fupplied the poor family with neceffaries, Mrs. Blandford ftopped at the
next town, where fhe hired a nurfe to
attend on the fick woman, and engaged
an apothecary to vifit her and the children. Before all this could be completed,
the night was advanced when they arrived at Mrs. Blandford's home—Perkly
feemed to wifh to be invited to ftay;
but, wearied by his attempts at wit, and
                              difgufted

difgufted by the many proofs fhe had
feen of real infenfibility, under the affectation of refined fentimentality, Mrs.
Blandford made no pretence of wifhing
his prefence. Having ftrutted about
therefore a quarter of an hour, and
affected to admire her houfe and garden, he departed, as he faid, for the
abode of a friend, about four miles
nearer London, who had given him a
preffing invitation to ftay fome time;
while Mrs. Blandford, fatigued with her
excurfion, was confoled for her loft
time by the confideration that fhe had,
in confequence of it, found an opportunity effectually to relieve a diftreffed
family.—Azemia, extremely glad to find
herfelf once more in the comfortable
home of her benefactrefs, formed no
other

other wifh than that they might, during the reft of the fummer, have no invitation, or at leaft accept of none to leave it.

As to a mafquerade, fhe befought Mrs. Blandford, while they breakfafted the next morning, never to take her to another.—" It is," faid fhe in her broken Englifh, " fuch a melancholy fight to fee fuch a number of people making fimpletons of themfelves by way of trying at fomething extraordinary, which, after all, feems to amufe none of them. I could not help being quite forry to look at fome of them dreffed up fo little like reafonable beings, and fqueaking nonfenfe, with fuch deformed mafks on, that they feemed to try both

in

in their minds and perfons to libel human nature."

Sagacious reader!—and Oh! more
formidable critic! do not here fhut the
book, and exclaim that fuch reflections
are not in character, and never were
made by a girl of feventeen, and a
ftranger.—Confider whether, if they are
not natural, they are juft, and remember that the heroine of a novel is a pri-
vileged perfon, who is to do and endure what never was done or fuffered
in real life. She may faft four or five
days, or as long as Elizabeth Canning:
fhe may ride over hills, through
woods, and round lakes, nights and
days, and be no worfe at the end of her
journey, than if fhe had taken an airing

to

to Kenfington with her grandmother.;
and fhe may make refle&ions worthy
of a Lord Chancellor, or an Arch-
bifhop, though it is well known that
in a&ual life beautiful young ladies
very feldom refle& at all.

CHAP. IX.

So Pluto seized on Proserpine.

IT was two months after this time, and summer was gradually fading into autumn, when Mrs. Blandford was suddenly summoned to London to meet an old friend, who, after a long residence in the West Indies, had returned to England in so bad a state of health, that she was unable to leave London, as she was desired to do, for Bath; and finding herself daily become worse, she

desired

defired to fee her oldeft and beft friend,
and to give her fome directions about
her family, before fhe became too ill to
execute thefe tafks of duty and prudence.—Mrs. Blandford loft not a moment in obeying the fummons—it was
likely that fhe fhould be abfent only a
few days; and as Azemia wifhed rather
to remain, unlefs fhe could be ufeful,
and Mrs. Blandford was unwilling to
take her, it was agreed that fhe fhould
be left in the country.

Mrs. Blandford then departed; and
Azemia, who now found the advantage
of the refources fhe had acquired,
tafted reading well enough to amufe
herfelf many hours: then, the evening
being remarkably clofe and warm, fhe
ftrolled towards a fmall lawn that partly
                    furrounded

furrounded the houfe, but had hardly
proceeded many paces before a fervant
from the houfe, following her, informed
her Mr. Perkly was come, and defired
to fpeak to her.   Azemia difliked this
man at all times, but particularly difliked to fee him in the abfence of Mrs.
Blandford: fhe was not, however, well
enough acquainted with the numerous
ways there are of efcaping importunate
vifitors, and therefore returned, though
reluctantly, into the houfe, where Perkly
had vifited three or four times fince
their meeting at Lady Buckray's, though
Mrs. Blandford had been very far from
giving him encouragement.—Azemia
now thought him more importunate and
difagreeable than ever; he afked a thoufand queftions, fuch as the name of the
lady to whom Mrs. Blandford was gone,

the ftreet where fhe lived, how long the vifit was likely to be, and many other interrogatories, which, though fhe always thought him impertinent, now feemed more fo than ever.

Azemia at length took courage to tell him, that as Mrs. Blandford was abfent, fhe could not afk him to ftay; and, with great fatisfaction, fhe faw him depart.

The next morning fhe went out to attend on fome India pheafants, for which a fmall wooded corner of the garden had been netted off; when fhe was furprifed by a note from Mrs. Blandford, written, as it feemed, in great diftrefs of mind. It was to inform her that her friend was worfe, and that, as

fhe

she was herself unwell, she could not dispense with the attendance of her dear Azemia; and begging that she would therefore set out for London immediately in her friend's post-chaise, which was sent for her. Azemia flew into the house, forgot all her dislike to going to London; and calling the housemaid to assist her in packing a few necessaries, (for Mrs. Blandford's own maid had accompanied her mistress) she was ready in a few moments; and, with a mind ill at ease on account of the indisposition of her beloved benefactress, got into the handsome post-chaise that waited, and, attended by a creditable servant in livery on horseback who had come with it, began her journey.

I 2   The

The day was exceſſively warm, and
their progreſs ſlow: Azemia þegan to
think it extremely tedious. The chaiſe
ſtopped at a little alehouſe by the road-
ſide to refreſh the horſes, and Azemia
ventured to enquire of the ſervant how
far they yet had to London. The man
aſſured her they would ſoon arrive
there; adding, as a reaſon for the time
they had taken, that, to avoid ſome
ſandy and hilly road, the poſtillion had
come round an eaſier way, which beſides
gave them the advantage of getting into
London by a quarter of the town nearer
to Mrs. Anderton's houſe, by which
means they would avoid going over the
ſtones for above a mile.

Azemia ſuppoſed all this perfeſtly
true; yet a ſenſe of the great difference
of

of the time taken up in this and her
former journey foon recurred to her
again, as flowly they travelled on in
very fhaking roads. The fun was now
funk; it became dark; and Azemia,
who had never till then had much idea
of fear, began to feel uncomfortable
when fhe reflected that fhe was alone
in a very lonely, and, as it now feemed,
in a fort of wild and woody country;
for fhe obferved by the twilight that
the carriage had left the road and en-
clofed lanes, and was driven over grafs
among thickets of trees: fhe thought
it neceffary to fpeak again; for, by all
fhe recollected of the approach to the
metropolis, nothing could be more unlike it than the place where they then
were. It was fome time before the
poftillion heard; and when, at laft, he

I 3   ftopped,

ſtopped, he anſwered ſomewhat ſullenly,
that it would not be long before they
got to the place where they were going
to. Azemia, ſtill more terrified, as well
by the man's rude anſwer as by obſerving they were going into a darker
part of the foreſt by a narrow road,
deſired to ſpeak with the other ſervant.
The poſtillion anſwered, in a yet more
ſurly way, that he was gone on before:
Azemia then aſked whither?—and if he
was gone to London?—The fellow made
no anſwer.

Impenetrable darkneſs now fell a-
round, and the road appeared to be ſo
bad, that the chaiſe was likely every
moment to be overturned: at length,
however, after being for about half an
hour ſhaken among ruts that threatened
diſlocated

diflocated limbs, the motion of the carriage became eafier; fhe faw lights move
about in a houfe before her, gates were
opened, and fhe was foon at the door,
where the fervant who had attended
her from Mrs. Blandford's opened the
door of the chaife, and defired her to
alight.—" Oh! pray," exclaimed fhe,
" tell me why I am brought hither?—
This is not London?—Mrs. Blandford
cannot be here ?"

No anfwer was returned: Azemia was
led into a large handfome room; a female fervant appeared—and, fpeaking
loud, as if becaufe fhe was a foreigner
fhe could not hear, faid that the
lady fhe belonged to would be there
to-morrow; that in the mean-time fhe
muft eat her fupper, and go to bed.

I 4 The

The woman spoke to Azemia exactly
as she would to a child of ten years old,
and seemed to assume an authority
which added to the alarm she had
already conceived—fears of she knew
not what. She spoke as well as she
could to the woman; but her appre-
hension occasioned her to express herself with more difficulty than usual, and
the only answer she obtained was—
" Ah! well, well; there, there—I don't
understand you. I warrant you ben't
much hurt in being brought to such a
house as this here. Come, Miss, no
whimpering!—What!—I wonders what
you have to complain on indeed!"

Azemia, finding her remonstrance of
no use, remained quiet; the woman
went away, and the fair young prisoner
began

began to explore the precincts to which she was confined.—The room wherein she was left opened by a large mahogany door into another still larger—it seemed to be magnificently furnished with large pictures; it was carpeted, and the curtains were of the richest damask, with gilt cornices. The candle Azemia held in her hand cast but a feeble light around so large an apartment; the doubtful obscurity dismayed her, and she returned, with light steps, to the room she had left, where a female servant, a sort of housekeeper, whom she had before seen, appeared, laid a cloth on a small table, and made signs to Azemia to seat herself, and to eat of the jellies, pastry, and fruit, with which it was covered.

I 5

Without

Without any diftinct notion of the caufes fhe might have for perfonal alarm, the greateft uneafinefs Azemia felt was on account of Mrs. Blandford. Why fhould fhe have written to her as fhe did? or if, as fhe began to fuppofe, there was any deception in it, for what purpofe, and by whom, could fhe have been thus drawn away from the protection of Mrs. Blandford? and what muft her beloved benefactrefs think when fhe learned that fhe was gone!

Thefe reflections, and the vague fears that tormented her, kept her waking the whole night on the bed of down to which fhe had been conducted. At the dawn of day, which fhe watched through the gilt window-fhutters and chintz curtains of her room, fhe arofe, and

and opened them. She faw that the
houfe on that fide was fituated in a large
and beautiful garden: a gravel walk,
bordered with variety of flowering
fhrubs and foreft trees, led round an
extenfive lawn to a canal edged with
weeping willow, and winding away till
it was loft among plantations apparently of confiderable extent. Azemia,
having dreffed herfelf, intended to go
down ftairs and walk in the pleafant
grounds fhe faw before her: but, on
attempting to leave her room, fhe found
the door locked; and in a few moments afterwards fhe was amazed and
alarmed by the appearance of Mifs
Sally!—a perfon who was almoft ex-
pelled from her recollection, but who
now, difagreeably enough, was recalled
to it. Her chubby white face feemed

I 6   fwelled.

swelled with malignant triumph: she addressed herself to Azemia with a sneering reproach for her escape, and treated her like a creature over whom she had obtained a right and might to dispose of as she pleased. Her manner was enough to overcome the spirits of the innocent girl, who, recollecting all that Mrs. Blandford had endeavoured to impress upon her mind as to the former conduct of this woman and of her first captor, was struck with dread of their present designs, and burst into tears.—Miss Sally, without feeling or pity, continued to exclaim on her ingratitude and her folly: she added—" However, Miss, you are now come back to those you belong to; you are far enough from the impertinent meddling old woman who chose to keep

                                    you

you from your right friends; and *they* will take care, I affure you, that you fhall not fet out on your travels again in a hurry."

Azemia, weeping bitterly, enquired if fhe might not be permitted to walk in the garden.—" Yes, yes, you fhall walk, never fear; but you'll have no opportunity here to walk away. Come, no whimpering—you'll fpoil your pretty eyes, Mifs: I advife you to make your-felf eafy, or, I affure you, it will be worfe for you."

To prevent my readers forming va-rious conjectures as to the prefent fitua-tion of *our* heroine, they are to know, that, at the mafquerade, a certain ce-

lebrated

lebrated Political Orator and Writer had
appeared as Peter the Hermit, while,
among other Crufaders and chivalrous
Knights affembled round him, was the
noble Duke mentioned in the firft part
of thefe memoirs, who forbore to un-
mafk the whole night, and whofe prefence was known only to the lady of
the houfe. He no fooner beheld Azemia, and difcovered that fhe was the
lovely Turk once an inmate of his houfe,
than he felt the moft unconquerable
wifh to get her again in his power.
Mr. Perkly had long been one of his
accommodating friends: he immediately
received inftructions to make an acquaintance with Mrs. Blandford, and
what had followed was by his contrivance. Azemia being a perfon belonging

longing to nobody, and kept, as was fuppofed, by Mrs. Blandford through charity, it was believed that none would think it worth while to enquire about her; or, if they did, that none poffeffed any right to reclaim her.

CHAP.

CHAP. X.

━━━━━━

From bad to worfe too oft the Sufferer falls,
    Yet let no Sufferer for that caufe defpair :
Good out of evil, Deftiny oft calls—
    Which we fee not—Alas ! how blind we are !

ANONYMOUS.

━━━━━━

THE amazement and confternation of
Mrs. Blandford, when fhe returned to
her own houfe, are not to be defcribed.
She made, in vain, every enquiry in
her power of her fervants, and then
every attempt to trace her unfortunate
ward, but all in vain : no perfon could
give

give any account of the chaife, or its attendants; and, in fact, it had been driven a crofs road, for near twenty miles, to the foreft on which this villa of the Duke's was fituated, though it was not much more than that diftance from London.

While Mrs. Blandford was tormented with the moft uneafy conjectures as to the fate of poor Azemia, which increafed in proportion as time went on, the noble owner of her prifon thought proper to vifit his beautiful prifoner.

Azemia, who had for fome days ceafed to regard the occafional infults of Mifs Sally, and was for the greateft part of her time left at liberty to walk

in

in the plantations, or amuſe herſelf as
ſhe choſe, and who ſaw no perſon appear to alarm her, was become more
tranquil; and, not knowing the pre-
cautions that had been taken to elude
all ſearch, flattered herſelf that Mrs.
Blandford would ſoon diſcover her, and
that ſhe ſhould once more be reſtored
to her protection. Her diſpoſition was
naturally cheerful and ſanguine; and her
imagination was uninfluenced by ſuch
reading as tells of

" Moving accidents by flood or field;"

ſhewing how damſels have been ſpirited
off, and ſhut up by ſundry evil-diſpoſed
gentlemen—a circumſtance which is
hardly omitted in any novel ſince the
confinement of Pamela at Mr. B—'s
houſe

houfe in Lincolnfhire, and the *enleve-
ment* of Mifs Byron by Sir Hargrave
Pollexfen.

Of all thofe hiftories, and of thofe
of modern romances, wherein ladies are
carried per force into caftles, and fcud
about woods by moonlight to efcape,
Azemia was happily ignorant; fo that
ideal grievances added but little, for
fome time, to the real one of being fe-
parated from Mrs. Blandford, and occafionally compelled to endure the imper-
tinence of Mifs Sally.

But when the venerable nobleman
arrived, and, confidering her as ignorant
even of the language he ufed, furveyed
her as he would a beautiful animal,
then with a moft ridiculous, yet difguft-
ing

ing expreſſion of admiration, approached and took her hand, Azemia became
immediately conſcious of the fate to
which ſhe was condemned, and, acquiring
at once courage to repel the inſults
which ſhe thought it would be too probable he might offer, told him in a
calmer tone than could be expected,
that ſhe inſiſted on being releaſed; that
no perſon had any right to detain her;
and that ſhe would inform Mrs. Blandford that he confined her contrary to
her inclination.

The Duke heard her with the ſort
of ſatisfaction with which one liſtens to
an amiable child, who, in its infantine
anger, ſhews unexpected marks of
ſtrength of mind. He ſeemed aſtoniſhed
at the progreſs ſhe had made in ſpeaking
Engliſh;

Englifh; and in a few days, from mere
liking to her beautiful form, he became
fo dotingly fond of her for the energy,
as he called it, of her mind, that he
no longer approached her but with
refpect; and inftead of the bafe intentions he had at firft harboured, he
appeared to be difpofed to end all his
follies by marrying this lovely Afiatic;
and would, perhaps, have done fo, if,
on one hand, he had not been pofitively engaged before to Lady Be-
linda, and to five equally amiable fair
ones; and on the other, if he had not
foon feen, that, while Azemia beheld
him with unconquerable averfion, fhe
was totally unmoved by, though fhe
perfectly underftood, the various ad-
vantages of fortune and rank he had
the power of offering her.

After

After ſtaying more than a week, the enamoured antiquity, who fancied himſelf more in love than he ever was in his life, returned to London, giving orders that Azemia might not be contradicted in any thing; that all which could amuſe and engage her might be ſupplied, and that ſhe might be allowed to walk in the garden whenever ſhe pleaſed—only that care ſhould be taken ſhe went no farther than about the grounds; which was altogether improbable, as they were ſurrounded on all ſides either by a wall, or a very high paling, within which was a wide and thick plantation of firs, other evergreens, and large trees; while without, next the foreſt, ad eep ditch ran all round beyond the paling. There was no entrance but by a lodge, where the porter knew how

how to obey the orders that were given him, too well to leave the leaſt doubt of the innocent priſoner's eſcape.

Miſs Sally, fatigued by a cloſe attendance as jailoreſs for almoſt three weeks, and occupied by ſome plans of her own, inſenſibly relaxed her vigilance; and a day or two after the Duke's departure Azemia was ſuffered to wander about as ſhe would. She returned regularly at the hours Miſs Sally expected to ſee her; and it was a relief to the latter not to be under the neceſſity of following her.

The doors of her apartment were now no longer locked; and one evening after ſhe had taken her ſlight repaſt, and retired to it, ſhe obſerved from the windows that the moon ſhone with uncommon

common luſtre : its glancing rays were
trembling on the canal, and among the
trees that waved over the lawn. Its chequered radiance gave a penſive ſweet-
neſs to the ſcene, which Azemia deſired
to enjoy in the open air.—The ſtairs
and paſſages were all carpeted, ſo that
her light footſteps were not heard by any
one ; and ſhe ſoftly unbarred the glaſs
door opening on the lawn, which opened
afterwards by a ſpring lock, of which
ſhe knew the ſecret.

With the feelings of a bird that has
regained a momentary liberty, Azemia
walked forth; for at all other times,
however far ſhe had rambled from
the houſe, ſhe always thought herſelf
watched. Now ſhe believed ſhe was
wholly unobſerved; and the pleaſure
that

that fuppofition gave her, counteracted
every fenfation of fear at the filence and
lonelinefs of the fcene, that fhe might
at another time have felt. Approaching the canal, fhe followed its winding
banks, and admired the effect of the
moon-beams trembling at intervals among
the trees on its furface, which was gently
curled and agitated by the night breeze,
as it fighed among the woods, that bent
and fwathed as it paffed them.

Azemia, loft in a pleafing fort of melancholy mufing, walked on towards the
darker parts of the lawn, where the trees
clofed over the broad grafs walk lead-
ing round to its extremity. No living
creatures feemed to be abroad but the
hares, which at firft ftartled her as
they darted acrofs her path, on being

disturbed by her approach. There were an infinite number encouraged and protected here by the noble owner of the domain, who would have punished a peasant, or petty farmer, more severely for destroying one of *them*, than for killing half a dozen parish children. Having observed above twenty of these innocent animals feeding or sporting among the shrubs, the sudden scudding of two or three almost over her feet no longer alarmed her: she even stepped more lightly, if possible, not to break in, even in their timid apprehensions, on the security they appeared to enjoy at this hour of silence, for it was midnight.

Re-assured as to any fears for herself by the perfect tranquillity of every object around her, Azemia, without any intention

intention of escaping (for to escape
seemed impossible), continued her way.
She now entered a darker and narrower
wood walk, almost at the extremity of
the plantation. Several cedars, and cu-
rious firs feathered down to the ground,
had an area cut round them to admit air,
while beyond them laurels and holly,
privet and phillyrea, formed beneath the
high elms and limes a screen of impenetrable darkness; and Azemia could
only see the moon among these recesses;
in the narrow parts it did not even en-
lighten the path before her. Suddenly,
as slowly she pursued her way, she was
somewhat startled by a shrill and often
repeated cry, not unlike that of a young
infant; it seemed almost close to her:
but before she had time to consider what
it might be, three men rushed out from

K 2   the

the dark thicket, and darted towards the
place from whence the cry feemed to
proceed. The fight of a human creature feemed to alarm the two laft, who
ftopped and evidently meant to impede
the paffage of the trembling Azemia;
while the third, who had more eagerly
purfued his game, ftepped from among
the coppice wood in half a moment, ex-
claiming with an oath—"I've got another, and a devilifh large one!"—He
held a hare in his hand; and feeing his
companions, who had by this time feized
on the half-dead Azemia, he joined in
their efforts to carry her out of the
grounds; which they prefently effected
by means of fome pales they had fo
loofened, that they could remove them
at their pleafure, and replaced fo as
that it could not be difcerned that they

were

were loofe.   Thefe three depredators of
the night had no difficulty in convey-
ing their light and almoft unrefifting
burthen acrofs the deep foffé furrounding the grounds; and Azemia was now
amidft the pathlefs wildernefs of an extenfive chace, in the power of three ruffians, one of whom was a notorious
footpad that had long infefted the roads
round London, and had retired among
perfons very little better than himfelf, to
fubfift with them on poaching and other
petty thefts, till the fearch made for
him in and about the metropolis, in confequence of a recent robbery and mur-
der, was a little abated: with them he
had affociated in fetting fnares for game,
and the cry Azemia heard was that of a
hare taken in a wire.

K 3   CHAP.

CHAP. XI.

———
———

What if our Heroine meet with dire mifchance,
Loft in the mazes of this tangled wood?

———
———

READER! if I now chofe, in this my concluding fection, to follow the example of a great mafter, and his ingenious copyift, I might gravely begin a long differtation, and difcourfe admirably and very much to the purpofe as to the probability of what I have juft made my heroine encounter. I will not—no, I pofitively will not take undue

advantage

advantage of your impatience to know
what becomes of my interesting Azemia. I will recollect how often I have
myself impatiently turned over, without
reading it, a profing digreffion, when
I was impatient to learn whether the fair
ideal creature, for whom I had fuffered
myfelf to be anxious during many
chequered pages, was killed or married
at their clofe.

Oh! ye amiable and graceful female
readers under twenty, who may perchance perufe this my firft effay " in the
novel line," as ye wait in your machine
till the Nereids in blue flannel at Mar-
gate or Brighton fhall wade towards
you in your turn; or who may take it
up in the parlour window while ye wait,
for your horfe, or your fociable—(for

K 4   now,

now, alas! the chance a novelift had of
being read as your hair was dreffed is
at an end)—ye will difpenfe with any
argument by which I can prove that
my heroine's adventure is extremely
probable, if I haften to relieve ye from
the pain your fufceptible bofoms muft
feel, when ye refleét on the fituation of
my fáir, young, innocent and beauteous
Azemia, in the hands of three ruffians,
in the midft of a wild foreft, in the
middle of the night, when nothing was
fo improbable as her being faved from
the horrors that awaited her.—To proceed then:

After the three men had carried her
out of the plantations, they began to
debate how they fhould difpofe of her
for the night; and he who was the

moſt daring, and of courſe had a ſort of
aſcendancy over the others, inſiſted
upon their helping him to convey her
to the lone cottage, where he was himſelf concealed, which was two miles
farther in the foreſt. To this the others
objected: but the fiercer wretch pulled
a piſtol from his pocket; and knowing
they were unarmed, except with hunting
poles pointed with iron, he ſwore that the
firſt of them that made any reſiſtance to
what he directed ſhould have a brace of
balls through his body. Azemia, who,
a little recovering, had fallen ſenſeleſs
on hearing this hideous wretch ſpeak as
he did, was borne between the two ſub-
ordinate men, who were only poachers;
the other, who was a ruffian of a much
more dangerous deſcription, following
them with his piſtol in his hand.

K 5   Several

Several cross roads interfected the foreft, all of which it was impoffible to avoid in going towards the place where the robber infifted on having his prey conveyed. They arrived at a broad green road, where the turf was but little marked by wheels, and were proceeding acrofs it, when the quick approach of horfemen ftartled them.—Confcious guilt generally creates cowardice. The youngeft of the men that bore Azemia let go his hold, and was prefently loft amid the thickeft wood: the other was about to confult his own fafety, and efcape alfo, when he was feized by the nervous arm of one of the horfemen, while a piftol difcharged by the ruffian was inftantly anfwered by the firing of a piftol by the other man on horfeback; and then leaping from his horfe, he cut

at

at him with an hanger he wore by his
side, and, closing with him, threw him
on the ground—but not till he had himself received a ball from another pistol
in his arm. The second poacher had
by this time disappeared; and the stranger,
ordering his companion, who was his
servant, to secure the fallen robber, ran
to the assistance of the female, who was
left lying on the ground, and who was
to all appearance dead.

What were the sensations of the brave
and fortunate champion of innocence in
distress, when he saw his Azemia—his
long lost, his adored Azemia! for know,
gentle reader, that this young hero was
no other than Charles Arnold himself.

K 6   It

It would be a vain attempt to deſcribe
the ſenſations that crowded on the heart
of the gallant young ſeaman, while he
thus held in his arms the lifeleſs form of
her whom he had ſought at every inter-
val of receſs from his duty, and never a
moment ceaſed to think of with paſ-
ſionate tenderneſs. His firſt apprehen-
ſions were that ſhe was dead—his firſt
hopes to bear away the lovely form from
the ruffians, whom he expected every
moment to return. He threw himſelf
upon the ground by her—ſpoke to her,
chafed her cold hands, and then attempted to raiſe her; his faithful ſervant was ſtill employed in ſecuring the
diſabled ruffian, who with dreadful exe-
crations ſtruggled to force himſelf from
the graſp of honeſt Bat.

" Tie

" Tie his hands behind him," cried
Arnold, " and haften to me, or it will be
too late to fave—to recover this lovely
creature." Bat, with difficulty, per-
formed this troublefome office ; and then
his mafter mounting his horfe, he lifted
Azemia into his arms ; and Bat, having
fecured the piftols that had been fcat-
tered around this fcene of fudden contention, followed on the other horfe.

Azemia, after a few moments, opened
her eyes, and Arnold, in the gentleft ac-
cents, endeavoured to prevent the éf-
fects of a too fudden furprife, while he
convinced her, that fhe was not only in
prefent fafety, but protected by her
fondeft, tendereft friend. Joy was the
momentary fenfation that affected the
heart of Azemia ; but it was too fud-

den

den and tumultuous to affift her in re-
gaining her ftrength. She poffeffed only
recollection enough to cling round the
neck of her deliverer, while her head
funk on his fhoulder; and in this fitua-
tion, after about an hour's journeying,
they arrived at the houfe of the uncle
of Charles Arnold, who lived about
fix miles from the place where he had
fo miraculoufly refcued Azemia from
the probability of a fate a thoufand
times worfe than death.

Arnold, who was always welcome at
his uncle's houfe, and had been ufed to
go thither whenever, arriving from fea,
he had a fhort leave of abfence, made no
fcruple of rapping loudly at the door;
where, however, they waited fome time
before the family were roufed. At length
the

the trufty old houfekeeper looked out
of the window; and hearing the voice
of Arnold, who was a great favourite
with every body in the houfe, fhe
called up the reft of the fervants, and
haftened down herfelf to open the
door.

This good gentlewoman, an ancient
fpinfter, who had been educated rather
above what is ufual in her ftation, was
amazed at feeing her mafter's nephew
appear, bearing between him and his
fervant a young woman, whofe uncommon beauty, notwithftanding the fitua-
tion fhe was in, gave the prudent houfekeeper the greateft alarm for the dif-
cretion of her young favourite, Mr.
Arnold.

Arnold,

Arnold, in a hurried voice, and somewhat impatiently, anfwered the queftions fhe put to him; then entreating her not to lofe a moment in talking, but to attend the young lady to a bed, and call up one of the maid fervants to affift in procuring what might be neceffary to her refrefhment and comfort, he flew to his uncle, and, awakening him without fcruple, related in a few words all that had happened—not difguifing from him, that the young creature he had fo providentially refcued was the fame Turkifh beauty who had, about fourteen months before, made fo deep an impreffion on his heart; for which, whenever they had fince met, his uncle had rallied him without mercy.

Mr.

Mr. Winyard (fo was this worthy man called) knew Charles Arnold too well to fuppofe, that, under this ftory, he concealed one of thofe frolics in which young men fometimes indulge themfelves; he therefore rang for his houfekeeper, and gave her ftrict orders to take the utmoft care of the young lady: then bidding his nephew attend to his own refrefhment and repofe (for he looked extremely pale and fatigued), the good man betook himfelf to recover his fleep, and poftponed till the next morning the enquiry that fomewhat puzzled him, by what ftrange chance a young woman could be found in the middle of the night in the power of three ruffians, and in fuch a place.

He

He knew nothing of the wound
Charles Arnold had received, or he
would have been much more difquieted.
Our hero was himfelf hardly fenfible of
it, while any thing remained to be done
in the fervice of Azemia : but as foon as
he found her completely reftored to her
recollection, and faw that fhe fhed tears
of gratitude to heaven, and to him, as the
immediate inftrument of her deliverance;
and when he afterwards learned from the
good houfekeeper that fhe was in bed,
had taken fome refrefhment, and feemed
quite calm and eafy, he began to feel
that fome attention was neceffary to himfelf; he therefore took off his coat, and
fummoned his faithful Bat to infpect his
wound, which the coldnefs of the night
had prevented from bleeding fo exceffively as it would otherwife have done.

Bat,

Bat, who was no unfkilful furgeon, having attended as Doctor's fervant in two
engagements, declared, after a flight ex-
amination, that he felt the bullet very
plain on the other fide of the arm,
through which it had paffed without
touching the bone.—" Cut it out then,"
cried his mafter; "cut away, my good
fellow, and let's have done with it, for
I have no time to nurfe it; and if I
fend for one of your regular-bred land
doctors, they'll make a job of it perhaps."—Bat, with the moft perfect *fang-
froid*, did as he was bid. Mrs. Gerkin,
the houfekeeper, was then called, who,
with a thoufand lack-a-days! and good-
neffes, and oh! dears! applied fuch re-
medies to the wound as her limited
knowledge of fuch matters made her
believe

believe would the most readily heal it;
and Arnold, whose life had within a
few hours obtained in his estimation
a greater value than he had ever set
on it before, was prudent enough to
forbear taking any thing stronger than
a little whey; after which he retired
to the bed that was always reserved
for him; but not to sleep; the strange
adventure of the night, and the joy
of having saved his Azemia, prevented him much more than the pain
of his wound from closing his eyes
till day-break; when, overcome with
fatigue, he sunk into temporary for-
getfulness, but soon started from it;
and as a confused remembrance of
what had passed recurred to him, he
eagerly asked himself if it was not
                                    all

all a dream, till the pain his arm
gave him affured him of its reality,
and for doing fo the fevereft pain he
could have endured would have been
welcome.

CHAP.

CHAP. XII.

———

"None but the Brave deferve the Fair."

———

IMPATIENT to enquire after Azemia, on whom he felt that his happinefs more than ever depended, Arnold
was at her door at eight o'clock, and
learned from the woman who had fat by
her bed-fide, that fhe had for fome hours
flept calmly, and had awaked greatly
refrefhed. Made happy by fo favour-
able an account, Arnold then haftened

to

to his uncle, whom he found already in his garden. The good man, who had never felt to excefs, and had long fince ceafed to feel the paffions that now agitated the bofom of his nephew, was a good deal difturbed by the vehemence of his manner, as well as by the extreme palenefs of his countenance. To make him eafy as to the latter, Arnold told him of his wound, affuring him at the fame time it would not be of the leaft confequence. Mr. Winyard, who loved his nephew more than any other perfon on earth, though he had four children of his own, was greatly alarmed, and infifted upon fending for the beft medical advice in the neighbourhood. Arnold, finding all oppofition in vain, confented, and the more readily, becaufe he thought it highly neceffary that the ftate of Aze-

mia's

mia's health, after fo great a fhock as
fhe had received the preceding evening, fhould be attended to.

Azemia, however, had already recovered herfelf much more than could
have been expected. Towards after-
noon fhe was able to rife ; and being ac-
commodated with a change of clothes by
the houfekeeper (for Mr. Winyard's
daughter was married, and had left him
fome years), fhe dreffed herfelf ; and her
native, untaught politenefs told her that
fhe could not too foon thank her prefent benefactors, nor inform her firft
benefactrefs of what was become of
her.

A meffage, defiring to fee them, brought
Arnold and his uncle to her. If he had
                                    thought

moſt lovely in the dreſs of her country, when he firſt ſaw her in the early bloom of youthful beauty, ſhe ſtruck him now as being even more beautiful and intereſting. The ruſtic ſimplicity of dreſs ſhe wore, (that of a grave old ſervant), her paleneſs, her languor, and the words, imperfect yet forcible, in which ſhe attempted to expreſs the grateful feelings of her heart, were all ſo many charms that ſerved to rivet more ſtrongly than ever the fetters that the enamoured ſailor had worn from the firſt day of their meeting.

Eager to know by what ſtrange accident ſhe had been ſo accompanied when he ſo fortunately met her in the foreſt, he deſired Azemia to explain to him what had happened to her ſince they laſt

met. Azemia endeavouring to collect
at once Englifh and courage enough to
go through it, though fhe had herfelf but
little idea of the real caufes that had in-
fluenced her various removals, Arnold
perfectly underftood them from her art-
lefs defcription of the perfons fhe had
been among. His indignation was particularly excited againft the old Captain,
her firft captor, who had, he thought, moft
bafely and ungeneroufly fold her to
fome man of rank, by means of the
woman with whom fhe had been placed.
Her laft efcape, however, which he
thought might poffibly be from the fame
man who had thus at firft purchafed
her, fhocked him ftill more, and made
him apprehenfive for her future fafety.
But towards Mrs. Blandford he felt the
livelieft gratitude; and upon Azemia's
mentioning

mentioning how much she wished that
excellent friend to know she was in
safety, Arnold, knowing she would be
perfectly secure in the protection of his
uncle, expressed an eager desire to go to
her himself. But this his uncle absolutely
forbade; for, though the distance across
the country was not more than thirty
miles, his recent wound made even so
short a journey extremely imprudent.

Honest Bat was, however, immediately dispatched, and directed to take
a man or two with him from the nearest
village, to the scene of their combat
with the poachers, and enquire into the
fate of the wretch whom they had left
wounded on the ground.

L 2   No

No traces of him could be found; and it feemed certain that, being lefs feverely hurt than they had imagined, he had found means to loofen his hands, and efcape to fome hiding-place amid the thickets of the foreft. Bat therefore, vowing vengeance againft this felon if ever he met with him again, proceeded to the houfe of Mrs. Blandford with a letter from Charles Arnold.

That excellent woman had fuffered fo much uneafinefs during the three weeks fince Azemia had been unaccountably betrayed from her protection, that fhe was now too ill to have left her home on any occafion lefs interefting than that of feeing and having her lovely ward reftored to her.—She now hefitated

fitated only till the next day. On account of the danger of travelling late
the road she was to go, she set out
attended by two servants armed, besides
Bat, who, as he led the way through
the forest, pointed, with some degree of
triumph, to that part of it where he and
his master had put to flight and dif-
comfited three stouter men than themselves.

While at Cherbury (which was the
name of Mrs. Winyard's house), Azemia and Arnold waited the return of the
messenger sent to Mrs. Blandford. Arnold, delighted that Azemia could now
understand him, made the best use of
his time to express to her the sentiments he felt for her. Azemia, who
had never seen any human creatures

L 3   that

that she loved, since her residence in England, but Mrs. Blandford and Arnold, had no more notion of disguising her affection for one of them than for the other: she therefore frankly told him, that, attached to him both by choice and by gratitude, she desired him to be assured, that she wished for no happier destiny than to be united to him according to the laws of his country, and to shew him, through life, the gratitude and tenderness of her heart.

Her ignorance of the modes and manners of a country where every circumstance differed so materially from her own, made her look forward to their future union without any of those anxieties that clouded the happiness of Charles Arnold.

Unfortunately,

and about two hundred pounds in prize-
money, to marry Azemia? He will
never hear of it: yet to relinquifh her
I feel to be impoffible.—I dare not,
however, now venture to fpeak of it."

The arrival of Mrs. Blandford was a
comfort to Azemia beyond all fhe had
ever felt; and her benefactrefs, liften-
ing to a detail of all fhe had fuffered,
could never be enough thankful to
Heaven, that had fo miraculoufly directed her firft acquaintance in England
to her refcue in a moment of fuch extreme peril.

It was difficult for the coldeft-hearted
perfon to be long with Charles Arnold
without loving him. The fweetnefs of
his temper moderating the ardour of his

L 5　　　　　　fpirits,

ſpirits, and the manly good-nature which marked his character, particularly endeared him to Mrs. Blandford; and after two or three days, when Azemia was ſo far recovered as to make her protectreſs ſuppoſe ſhe might undertake the journey home, Arnold at length acquired courage to tell her (what ſhe was well aware of before) that he was diſtractedly in love with Azemia, and wiſhed, notwithſtanding the ſlenderneſs, or rather nothingneſs, of his fortune, to marry her.—Obſerving that Mrs. Blandford liſtened to him without any marks of diſpleaſure, he proceeded with more courage to repreſent that her beauty, her youth, and the ſingular and unfortunate circumſtance of her belonging to nobody, would occaſion her to be continually expoſed, even under Mrs. Blandford's

Blandford's protection, to dangers of the fame nature as that fhe had already efcaped : in fhort, he pleaded fo well, and the generous nature of Mrs. Bland-ford fo well difpofed her to admit his arguments, that, after hearing what were his profpects (wherein he related fimply the truth), fhe told him, that though the principal part of her income was for life, fince fhe had now no children, fhe had a fum of about four thoufand pounds in the funds, which it had always been her intention to give to Azemia, fince fhe had no relations who either wanted or deferved it. This, therefore, fhe would immediately fettle upon her ; and till preferment in his profeffion, or fome other lucky chance, gave him greater affluence, Azemia fhould continue to live with her, where he alfo fhould

L 6

always find a home whenever he was
on fhore.

With a heart overflowing with joy
and gratitude, Arnold then flew to his
uncle, and eagerly communicated this
unexpected profpect of happinefs.—Mr.
Winyard, who was delighted, with his
vifitors, and already confidered Azemia
as his daughter, told him, that, though
he had three fons and a daughter of his
own, they being all provided for, he
had, thefe laft two or three years, been
laying by a little fund for the nephew
he loved.—" I have fcraped together
about fifteen hundred pounds, my dear
boy," faid he : " I give it you rather
before my death than after, that I may
be repaid by feeing you enjoy it. Marry
the woman you love, be as good a lad

as

as you have hitherto been, and never doubt but you will do well."

Parties being thus agreed, no unnecessary delay was created; and in lefs than a month from her fortunate refcue Azemia returned to the houfe of Mrs. Blandford as the wife of Charles Arnold.—He was foon obliged to leave her, to return to the duties of his profeffion; in which he foon after fo eminently fignalized himfelf, that he paffed rapidly through the intermediate fteps, and obtained a fhip.

His frequent abfences were the only circumftances that gave an alloy to the happinefs he enjoyed with Azemia; and while Mrs. Blandford and Mr. Winyard had the fatisfaction to contemplate,

as

as their own work, the felicity of thefe
deferving young people, I take leave of
my readers with this agreeable impreffion on their minds, and heartily hope
that many of them have met with fuch
good folks as thefe laft. I cannot fay I
have yet been fo fortunate myfelf; but
if I do not alarm my amiable young
countrymen too much by thus appearing in the character of a writing lady,
I do not defpair of fucceeding fo well
in my literary career as to make a
pretty little addition to my fortune;
with which (if it did not look too much
like advertifing for a hufband), I would
intimate, that I fhould be fuperlatively
bleffed to contribute to the happinefs
of fome tender, yet fenfible youth, who,
could be content with rural felicity in
an elegant cottage in Wales (for Bellegrove,

grove Priory is the inheritance of my elder brother); which cottage, with the profits of this work, I propofe to fit up in the moft elegant ftyle—and doubt not but, in time, it may humbly emulate that of the juftly celebrated Llangollen.

TO THE

REVIEWERS OF ALL THE REVIEWS;

ALL THE MAGAZINES;

AND

ALL THE NEWSPAPERS.

GENTLEMEN,

FROM being in habits of reading for many years your monthly lucubrations, to an infirm female relation who formerly lived in the literary world, I have ever since I was thirteen been inspired with the most ardent ambition to see myself spoken of favourably in every one of your pages, replete as they are with

discriminating

difcriminating knowledge and refined tafte. I know, gentlemen, your chafte impartiality, and am well aware, that you never fuffer either the rank or fituation of an author to influence you: you never give undeferved praife to any work, becaufe you are perfonally acquainted with the writer; or fpeak well of a performance utterly contemptible, becaufe your Review is edited by the publifher of fuch performance. Party, which has fo much effect in this our beloved country, that it fometimes fets the father at enmity with his fon, and divides the brethren of the fame houfe, never, I know, induces any of you to make the fmalleft variation in your rectitude. In a word, gentlemen, as I know nothing fo deftructive to a young author as your difapprobation, fo I feel that

your

your commendation is the acme of my aspiring hopes.

As a young artist studies with indefatigable perseverance the most celebrated models in sculpture or painting; so I, to avoid the common error of becoming a Mannerist, and to attain the felicity of

"Transplanting one by one into my work
"Their several beauties, till I shine like them,"

have studied with unwearied attention *all* the most approved novels of this present as well as the past day. You will not think me a plagiarist, when I declare that I have taken from the immortal Fielding, in one chapter, almost word for word; and trust I am, at least, in that passage, as *much* like him as *he* was

to.

to Cervantes. If I have omitted the incomparable Richardson, it was because my narrow limits would not allow me to describe, with his exquisite minuteness, the Cedar parlour, and Grand-mama's great chair; nor could I, by any means, though my Heroine weeps now and then, continue to bring my Hero to wipe her eyes *with her own handkerchief*, and *bow* upon her hand.

To attain the masculine force and strong colouring of the great Dramatist and Novelist of the present day, Mr. Cumberland, was quite beyond my slender attainment; but I have paid a due tribute to his taste, sagacity, and knowledge of *womankind*. Thrown at a great distance from the most engaging models among my own sex, I yet look up with

more

more confidence to attain, at some future day, a seat on that point of Par-
naſſus where they hold ſuch eminent
rank.   In this hope I have ſometimes
aſſumed the ſtately ſtep with which the
pupils of the Burney ſchool follow in
ſolemn, yet *inadequate* march, *their ini-
mitable leader. This,* however, I have attempted in *ſtyle* only.   I have not ſeen
enough of the world to ſketch even in
the way of a ſcholar, ſuch admirable
charaɛters.   With leſs diffidence, though
ſtill with great humility, I have ventured
with ſhuddering feet into the World
of Spirits, in modeſt emulation of the
ſoul-petrifying Ratcliffe—but, alas!

   " Within that circle none dare walk but ſhe."

Even if I *had* ever had the fortune to
ſee a *real natural ghoſt,* I could never
.deſcribe

defcribe it with half the terrific appa-
ratus that fair Magician can conjure
up in fome dozen or two of pages, interfperfed with convents, arches, pillars,
cypreffes, and banditti-bearing cliffs,
beetling over yawning and fepulchral
caverns. Her pictures,

" Dark as Pouffin, and as Salvator wild,"

can only be faintly copied;—to rival,
them is impoffible.—I own I do *not*
feel quite fo difheartened, when I try at
making fomething like the luminous
page of Mrs. Mary Robinfon: I even
flatter myfelf that I have, in more than
one inftance, caught the *air of probability* fo remarkable in her delectable
hiftories, as well as her glowing defcription and applicable metaphors.

To

To Mrs. Gunning's Novels, and those of her amiable daughter, I owe all in these little volumes that pretends to draw the characters and manners of high life. With due humility and trepidation I have seized the mimic pencil: I feel that I cannot wield it with their happy freedom and felicity—*faut d'ufage.*

To be insensible to the universal knowledge of the accomplished *Italian Traveller*, the attractive friend of *the Leviathan of Literature*, would be to want taste enough to value the glory of my sex. But the extensive erudition of that lady, grasping at all that literature and science can give; her elegant defultory gaiety; her elaborate research; her acute remarks; her erudite judgment;

ment; and, above all, her political candour, are as much above *my* praife as fuperior to *my* attainment.

From the parterres of Mifs Lee, Mrs. Inchbald, and Mrs. Smith, I have culled here and there a flower; and I fhould have enlarged my bouquet with buds and bloffoms of other very agreeable writers, of whom I could make (like Mr. Pratt) a very refpectable lift, if I could have induced my publifher to have allowed my work to be enlarged to what I intended it, viz. fix *very* large volumes. He affured me that it was too much for a *debut*; that my head was not yet furnifhed enough to fupply fo capital a work with ftory, fcenery, incident, character, dialogue, reflection, and all the various articles

neceffary

neceffary for an Epic in profe. I do
not, however, defpair (if you, Gentlemen, light me on my way up to the
fummit of Fame) of producing here-
after, *feven very large volumes* thickly
printed, duly interfperfed with pieces of
poetry, fuperior to what I have now
fown with extreme diffidence in the
prefent volumes—Volumes, Gentlemen,
which I offer you as my firft imitative
Effay—And (to finifh this fentence in
the *manner* of the *fweetly, the foftly fufceptible author of the meek and mild novel
of " Julia,"*) I have, in this work, like
the mocking-bird of the American wildernefs, caught with emulative ambition the dulcet notes of the harmonious
chorifters around me: the attempt is
exhilarating to the youthful fancy; and
fhe who at once attends to admonition,

and attempts excellence, though she may never equal the delicious *trills* of the Poet's beloved nightingale, may yet soothe the ear of the candid listener; and, if she does not soar into the empyrean with the lark, may at least enliven the hawthorn with the finch, or the orchard with the linnet!

Ah! Gentlemen Reviewers! Critics! by what name soe'er ye love to be invoked, do not crush my ambition in the shell; let it unfold, and, like the little Nautilus, float buoyant on the sea of public favour; be your animating *puffs* extended as well to me as to others of my sister Historians—Suffer me to

" Enjoy the triumph, and partake the gale."

To change the metaphor—do not blight with ungenial gales these efforts of bud-

.ding

ding genius—drive them not back into their *hybernacle*, by the chilling frosts of Criticisms. If I have faults, ye will tenderly hint at them—if I have *merit*, praise it; but I know you will, all of you, Gentlemen Reviewers by profession! for some of you are my particular friends, others are old acquaintances of my dear Grandmama, (who, good old Lady, used now and then to *do* an article herself, particularly in the British Critic)— To all of you I will send copies of my work.

Besides, ye are so tender-hearted, that ye will consider the tremors, the trembling breathless solicitude of a young beginner.—With what eagerness shall I, after my work is published, run over the list of " *Contents*" on your blue co-

vers! and when, Oh! moment of trepidation! " Jenks's Azemia" meets my
eye, with what impatience fhall I tear
open the important page on which the
fate of my literary life depends!

Suffer me to enjoy, by anticipation,
the praifes I am fure you will give me.——
Seven or eight months, perhaps, may
firft elapfe, and my work may be in a
third or fourth edition, before I fhall
read thus in ›

THE MONTHLY REVIEW.

" Modern Novelifts may be faid to poffefs
" their principal fhare of excellence in an artful
" conftruction of their *fables*. That a happy
" combination of ftory is neceffary we do not
" attempt to deny, but we think many other
" circumftances equally fo : thus character is
                                    undoubtedly

" undoubtedly one of the firſt requiſites. In this
" we know not whether the fair Authoreſs of
" Azemia has not failed.   Captain Wapping-
" ſhot is a mere ſketch, caricatured on ſome of
" the various Sea Characters ably delineated
" by Mr. Cumberland; but, upon the whole,
" this young lady's drawing is ſufficiently
" correct : the ſentiments ſhe puts into the
" mouths of ſome of her characters are ap-
" propriate and natural ;—the poetry inter-
" ſperſed in theſe little volumes is lively and
" agreeable.   We are ſorry our limits do not
" allow us to gratify our readers with a ſpe-
" cimen."

———

Thank ye, Gentlemen, a thouſand
times : this diſcriminating, calm praiſe
is juſt that temperate medium to rear a
nurſling of the Muſes.

M 3   Now,

Now, then, ye sterner, but not less
sagacious personages, who oblige the
world with

THE CRITICAL REVIEW.

"We are here presented with the first
"essay of a very young lady, who, it must be
"allowed, gives some proofs of not being
"totally destitute of genius. We disapprove,
"however, of the episode introduced at the
"end of the first volume: such tales are cal-
"culated to impress terror on young minds,
"and multiply, by imaginary evils, the real
"evils of life; whereas the business of the
"Novelist should be to recommend fortitude
"and prudent resolution. We think this
"lady's verse, in many instances, better than
"her prose :—the sentiments she expresses, as
"to the condition of the poor *under existing*
"*circumstances*, do honour to her heart. We
"have

" have no doubt but that a little more expe-
" rience in writing (which we think fhe will
" do well to endeavour at acquiring) will
" render this young lady's writing no con-
" temptible addition to the *firft* rank of the
" *fecond clafs of Modern Novels* :—at prefent
" we cannot place her higher."

———

Gentlemen, I acknowledge ye have
dealt honourably by me, and I will take
your advice; I will acquire experience
as faft as poffible.———Now for

THE ANALYTICAL.

To be analyfed, and fo feverely too!
Heavens! here *are* authors who would
almoft prefer annihilation—but I am of

M 4   better

better heart. Perhaps thefe Gentlemen may have no objection to ghofts, or ra- ther to the fhadows of fhades.—*Voyons.*

" This lady, who is, by her own account,
" a novice in the line of Novel-writing, feems
" to poffefs a fmall fhare of that uncommon
" talent for exhibiting, with picturefque
" touches of genius, the vague and horrid
" fhapes which imagination bodies forth, that
" has rendered another lady fo defervedly ce-
" lebrated. Her mode of telling the ftory
" of ' another Blue Beard,' reminded us,
" *faintly*, of Mrs. Ratcliffe. The nature of
" the work obliges us to digeft improbabili-
" ties, of which there are feveral ftriking
" inftances in the progrefs of the ftory, as well
" as in the before-mentioned epifode. We
" cannot help wifhing, in regard to the latter,
" that fhe had accounted for the fupernatural
" appearances in the *natural* and *probable* man-
" ner of her juftly-celebrated prototype. As it
" is,

" is, we are obliged to have recourse to an-
" cient legends, relative to *immaterialifm*,
" which are *entirely exploded*, and which *we*
" *are forry to fee revived in any book of rational*
" *entertainment.*

." In general we approve of this writer's
" fentiments; of which the following is no
" unfavourable fpecimen."

Here follows a quotation.——And,
again:

" Of our Author's defcriptive powers we
" fhall take the fcene in volume the firft, im-
" mediately after the departure of her lover:
" of the Poetry, the lines from ' the For-
" ficularis to her Love,' are the beft."

———

I make my courtefy to you alfo, Gentlemen, and then, with a fort of tender
confidence,

confidence, as a daughter, or a ward,
addrefs myfelf to *you*, ye *Britifh Critics*—my dear Grandmama's old worthy friends. Methinks I fee ye, venerable arbiters of tafte! I fee ye of both fexes (as my friend, Lady Harriet, fays ye are of each, fome male and fome female, and truly I believe it)—I fee ye, in *deep divan*, fitting with folemnity on my work :—your fecretary takes his pen —a refpectable matron—for with you, as the age of chivalry ftill exifts, it is always " *Places aux Dames*"—I fee her, (her cap a little on one fide by accident, which adds to the fagacity of her countenance) and I hear her dictating thus :—

" We congratulate the Novel-reading world
" on the acquifition of the fair Author of this
pleafing

" pleafing work, as an amiable labourer in the
" vineyard. She is, undoubtedly, a young
" lady of the firft promife ; and, if our *illuf-*
" *trious Premier* were not fuperior to all com-
" parifon, as he is exalted above all praife,
" we fhould have a flight degree of envy at his
" being honoured with fuch a panegyrift :
" but his *eximious* merit deferves that all the
" talents of the Britifh nation fhould be united
" in loud acclaim."

The venerable Lady here refigns her
dictatorfhip to a Reverend Divine.

" If it were poffible to make any objection
" to a work, the beauties of which would
" 'ftrike us blind' to its defects, were they
" more numerous, we might *juft hint*, that
" Mifs Jenks fhould have been more minute
" in her defcription of Azemia's baptifm ;
" whether *the fees* for that facred ceremony
" were duly paid, *who were the fponfors*, and
" in

" in what *parish* the fair creature, *thus rescued*
" *from Mahometism, was registered* : the pow-
" ers of our Authoress would have shone, in
" describing *the dinner* given, and the emotions
" of the beauteous convert *on that* occasion."

Here the man of the church resigns
his place, and is succeeded by a *Lay
Brother*, who holds a comfortable sine-
cure under Government.——This sage
Reviewer observes :

" If we were disposed to cavil at any thing
" in a book where there is so much right,
" and as it ought to be, *we* might hint that
" there are *some* passages, which the evil dis-
" posed might construe into reflections on the
" manners of the upper ranks of society—a
" style which, at this period, should by no
" means be admitted by any lover of good
" order ; nor can *we*, with all our esteem for
" Miss Jenks (with whose honourable family
" we

" we have long been connected), help advising
" her never to make the personages of her
" hiftory (even when fpeaking in character)
" retail common-place, we might almoft fay,
" Jacobinical common-place, on the condi-
" tion of the poor.—To our certain knowledge
" *no ground for any fuch remark does exift,* or
" *can exift,* under the prefent *happy, fortunate,*
" *flourifhing,* and *glorious ftate of this country.*

" We were extremely amufed with the
" Charades, though we could difcover *le mot*
" of the *firft* only, which we had indeed before
" heard accidentally.—We will not deprive
" our readers of the pleafure of guefling at the
" fenfe of this very ingenious effort of elegant
" female talent."

THE END.

BOOKS just published by SAMPSON LOW,
No. 7, BERWICK STREET, SOHO.